Snowed In at Snowcap Café

Jennifer Aline

PART OF THE HOLLY HILL
WINTER NOVELLA COLLECTION

Dedication

To all those who live for cozy winter nights.

To all those who live for snow days.

To all those who love espresso.

This one's for you.

And to my brother, Matthew. I will forever dedicate every book I write to you. Thank you for always pushing me to create, imagine, and write from the heart.

Content Warnings

- Explicit sexual content

- Mourning of a cell phone

- Curse words

- Overuse of "L" names

- Car accident (not on page)

- Incorrect use of espresso (...or maybe used correctly)

- Death of parents (not on page)

- INTENSE SIPPING...like, a lot. You've been warned.

welcome to
HOLLY HILL
SNOWCAP CAFE
219
MAIN STREET
HOLLY PEAK HWY
Holly Peak
the cabin

CHAPTER ONE

Alice

"TWO LARGE PEPPERMINT MOCHAS with almond milk! Sorry, all, but the peppermint syrup is officially *donzo*," I sang, lifting the to-go cups in the air and noticing another cup still sitting on the counter. Squinting down at my messy writing on the side of the cup, I added, "And one *super* dirty chai latte with two shots of espresso."

Two women wearing matching beanies snagged their peppermint mochas with a giggle before pulling up the hoods of their puffer jackets. I knew what was coming the second they reached for the handle of the front door, the bell jingling above. A gust of icy air engulfed the coffee shop when they pulled that door open, angry flakes flying across the welcome mat.

Holly Hill was known for this kind of weather. I'd lived here all my life and seemed to grow an extra layer of protection when it came to these elements. That, or I was just numb to it all at this point.

I mean, an early holiday season meant an early rush of snow bunnies and ski bums at our bed and breakfasts and cabin rentals. The more people who called Holly Hill their home during winter didn't *just* mean more customers at Snowcap Café, but more holiday cheer in general.

I couldn't be the only cheery one around here—or, at least, the only one *pretending* to be cheery.

Okay, that was a *little* dramatic. It wasn't that I put on an act, per se, because I did genuinely love the holidays. I lived for the smell of fresh brew as it sifted through the air of the shop—the scent of gingerbread and sugar cookie smacking customers lovingly in the face as they walked inside. I loved how awkward customers felt when carolers stopped at the shop door, their voices bouncing off the walls through a mix of applause and embarrassment.

It was just exhausting playing the part of *cheerful barista* without the original cheerful team behind me, tinkering at the espresso machine or memorizing the orders of regulars. I missed seeing the little sketches of Santas and reindeer sprinkling the cups. It was tough not hearing their laughs echo around me as I started another pour over or they corrected someone's order the way they always would.

It wasn't that I couldn't be cheery.

I just knew what it felt like when holiday cheer wasn't forced.

I knew how it felt when the holiday spirit came to life around you.

"I'm still looking for...uh..." I looked down at the to-go cup sitting on the counter, trying to decipher the name on the side. "Umm...Levi, maybe? Lorenzo? You're delectably *dirty* chai is ready for you!"

If only it hadn't been so busy ten minutes ago. I could have memorized the customer's facial features, hair color, and body language all in a matter of the minute it took to place an order. However, being the only barista working at the only coffee shop in Holly Hill made it so my multitasking skills were in overdrive.

I needed to hire a more reliable team.

The employees had been so inconsistent over the last three years.

Nothing beat the original three.

The door flew open as more customers walked outside into a wall of white, the cold clinging to my skin just as ring-covered hands slammed down onto the counter beside the lone chai. I didn't even need to look up to know who stood in front of me, out of breath, with pointed nails tapping.

Was she *really that* out of breath after walking from the corner booth to the counter?

Her corner booth?

It *had* to be anxiety.

"There's a travel ban, Al!" Dana whispered at a volume that wasn't really a whisper at all. She looked over her shoulder at the whitened windows before leaning in closer. "It's hella bad out there. Like...*bad.*"

Yup. It was *definitely* anxiety.

She flung her phone into my line of sight, the screen bright with bold, red words that did, indeed, say: *A State of Emergency and travel ban is effective immediately in Holly Hill and will remain until further notice. This ban is due to poor visibility and unsafe driving conditions as well as bitterly low temperatures that could lead to hypothermia and/or frostbite.* "Holly Hill hasn't had a travel ban in, like, two years! You have to kick everyone out, Al."

"Do you think it'll *seriously* be as bad as they make it out to be? The meteorologists here are *so* dramatic sometimes," I said, flapping my own ringed hand in her direction as beaded, bangled bracelets clinked together. Once a month, I hosted a local vendor market where nearby artisans sold their crafts, and jewelry, and in Dana's case, her smutty romance novels. The two of us were huge fans of one specific vendor, and we always bought way more jewelry than we could afford.

I peered down at my decorated fingers and wrists.

I regretted nothing.

"I don't know, Al..." Dana peered over her shoulder again at the curtain of white so heavy that the Holly Peak wasn't even visible anymore. She tapped her fingers against the reclaimed-wood countertop and said, "I think this is going to be a bad one."

I shooed my hands in her direction. "Then go home, woman! I need to wait for Lee, or Lawson, or Lindbergh to come get his chai before cleaning up."

"You're getting *real* creative with those L names now...but I kind of like Lindbergh the most." Dana gathered her laptop and notebooks from her corner booth. "Maybe Lindy will be a character in next fall's release."

"The one you'll be writing when you're out living the life in Luna Falls? Far, far away from the bitter cold."

"It's two hours from here, Al. We will get snowed on constantly in the winter. It's not like I'm leaving you to go on one of the *Rom-Com Ready* dating shows to write at some tropical island...even though that doesn't sound half bad." Dana's shoulders grew limp. "And you can't do that to me. The guilt trip plus your puppy-dog eyes won't help me convince myself the choice is a good one."

It was a little painful pushing out a genuine smile at the thought of my best friend leaving town in the spring. "It's a great opportunity. The choice is a good one," I admitted to her as she pushed open the front door, smiled, and raced into the night.

She wasn't one for goodbyes.

Whether short-term or long.

I looked down at the lonely chai by my hands. Other than a couple cleaning up their things and a woman—with the brightest damn ski pants I'd ever seen sticking out of her backpack—the shop seemed pretty damn empty. I wondered if that woman was still going to brave the mountain in this weather, since it looked like she was packed and ready to go. From what I could remember, her name didn't start with an L and from where I stood, her cup definitely looked empty. I was sure the couple by the window hadn't ordered the chai, so maybe the customer left in a blizzard-induced panic once the travel ban alert went off.

Then, I noticed Backpack-Pants was at the counter, her face definitely not giving off any hint of cheer.

"Done already?" I asked.

"Yep. Do you have a room where I can change?"

I looked back toward the closed bathroom door and then over her shoulder at the curtain of white covering the windows. "You can sneak into the bathroom or the break room if you want."

She whipped past me as if she'd never even asked the question, leaving her empty cup by the tablet as I took out the cash box to organize before closing—my least favorite part of owning the business. The door opened and closed again, the remaining couple walking out as a gust of icy air made a few dollar bills scatter on the floor. A blur of color flashed by me as I picked up the bills, and I realized it was the pants from Backpack-Pant's backpack.

Talk about a tongue-twister nickname.

Why did I do this to myself?

Startled but intrigued, I stated, "Those pants are interesting."

Her face didn't twitch with any form of a smile.

She was definitely my grumpiest customer of the day.

She quickly mentioned how she was, in fact, braving the ski hill, and as she exited the shop, I worried for her safety. Holly Hill weather was absolutely no joke. Even though she seemed tough as nails—or maybe her personality just was—going up that mountain during a travel ban would probably piss ski patrol off, and she'd piss herself off if she got hurt.

I cared too much about the well-being of strangers—even the grumpy ones.

It was both a blessing and curse of being a barista.

I jumped as wind shook the glass by the front door, and I rushed over to lock the doors and officially start closing up. I'd deal with the more *laborious* work tomorrow. Hauling bags of garbage through the snowstorm to the dumpster right now did *not* sound appealing, and since I was my own boss, I wasn't going to. What I *was* going to do was get the garbage from the bathroom, chuck it next to the front door, and then dive into bed with Archibald's scruffy little body warming my cold one.

The bathroom was somewhat hidden in the back of the shop, set into a nook of sorts. For some reason, people would stop looking once they got halfway there, turn around, and ask again where the bathroom was. It always struck me as odd because the shop was *not* big, by any means, nor was it dark and dingy. You were transported to a log cabin in the middle of the woods with a fireplace warming your toes near the entrance. Reclaimed-wood tables and cushioned benches scattered the space, with different colored pillows and blankets at each table for customers to cocoon into. Washing those blankets daily was pure hell, but my parents had made sure this space felt and looked straight out of a cozy, cinematic cabin in the woods, and I would forever continue their vision.

So, when people came to me, asking where the bathroom was, I was always a little confused. I'd tell them to walk beyond the fireplace and follow the art on the wall. I always hoped people would wander all the way to the back of the shop to look at the art-strewn walls and bright tapestries local artists donated.

I guessed most people saved their adventure for the mountain.

But my adventure for the night would end once I yanked out this damn bathroom garbage. Wrapping a ringed hand around the bathroom door handle, I pushed it forward.

Then my breath hitched.

The scream I wanted to let out lodged in my throat.

I stumbled directly into the chest of a tall, broad man in a tailored blue suit. He had one hand wrapped around my waist to reflexively catch my fall as the other hand flew back to steady us against the wall.

And when that hand found the wall behind him, it steadied our stumbling bodies, but it did *not* stop his phone—his *very* pristine, top-of-the-line phone—from diving straight into the toilet.

We both stared as it sat at the bottom of the toilet bowl, his hand not shifting from its spot around my waist, as if I could fall at any second. When the screen went dark beneath the water, I hesitantly stepped away from him and looked up to meet his eyes.

Up.

Like, *really* up.

He had to be, like, ten feet tall.

Maybe the Yeti of Holly Hill wasn't just a myth after all.

"So…" I whispered, tapping my fingertips together in front of my face. "I'm guessing you're Leander?"

A single, well-groomed eyebrow lifted, and he removed the dark-framed glasses from his face with a sigh. "Excuse me?"

"Does your name start with an L?" I asked, completely ignoring the fact that this giant of a man was hiding out in my bathroom, and all of his connections now sat at the bottom of my toilet.

Instead, I remained cheerfully business-minded, as always.

My parents had engrained this trait in me.

He placed the glasses back on his face. "Liam."

Damn.

How had I forgotten that one?

"Liam…" I said, attempting a smile that didn't look as forced as it felt. "There's a travel ban…and your dirty chai is ready."

Chapter Two

Liam

WELL, *THAT* CONVERSATION WAS over.

I guess I was okay with it—I mean, I had no other choice but to be.

Nonstop calls had forced me to pull over during the drive because, apparently, no one could wait two hours for a damn answer when it came to our next production contract.

So, yeah. I was okay that discussion ended.

Production and planning at Rom-Com Ready Ventures never stopped during the holidays. The winter months made viewers stir-crazy. They wondered where we would host the next season of our dating show series—a series I *never* expected would take off the way it had five years ago. Because the series went so viral so quickly, not only were my duties becoming more stressful but also tougher each season.

How could I find a group of people to fit the niche of that season's show?

Where could we host the show without causing too much of a scene?

What unique element would I bring to this summer's season since we were known to highlight local businesses.

I could have stood in this dimly lit bathroom all night, arguing about next season's location and the other dating show competing with the timeframe we'd already set into place. However, it was hard to focus on anything—even my sunken cell phone—with a tiny, elven blonde standing inches away...calling me *Leander*?

Did this pixie lady have a bag of rice I could throw my phone into?

I stopped listening after she said, "There's a travel ban..."

Wait, what?

No. Fuck.

"A travel what?" I set my hands on her shoulders—my palms huge over her little frame—so I could sneak by her and get the hell out of this bathroom. Once I got to the front of the shop, I could have sworn she pulled down curtains over the windows when she was closing up.

But those weren't fabric curtains.

They were white curtains of the heaviest damn snow I'd ever seen.

"Your dirty chai, sir?" her voice chirped from behind me, my hand flying up in surprise and practically knocking the chai out of her grasp. Fumbling, she held it between her hands with a furrowed brow.

"Jesus...all I want to do is give this drink a home so I can figure out how to save your phone from the depths of my toilet."

Her hand slowly started moving toward me until the cup was pressed against my chest. Looking down at her tiny ringed fingers, I quickly grabbed the drink, fearing some would drip on my suit. Bringing the drink to my lips, my eyes still linked with her curious ones, I took the long-awaited sip.

Damn.

Like...damn.

This was *good*.

And for a coffee and chai and espresso snob like myself, that said something.

"Thanks," I said softly, taking another *lukewarm* gulp.

"You're *very* welcome!" she sang, hopping backward with her hands clasped in front of her chest.

Then, her previous statement smacked the forefront of my mind. "Fuck. The phone!" I set the chai on the counter and raced to the back of the shop, sliding into the bathroom and staring at the phone sitting at the bottom of the toilet.

I did *not* want to reach in there.

Even though I'd only been using the bathroom as an office space—and never even using the toilet—I would *not* reach into that damn bowl.

No way in hell.

Right as I started scanning the bathroom for something that could help, the elf appeared at the door, wearing bright-yellow rubber cleaning gloves. Without saying a single word, she marched into the bathroom, reached into the toilet, and plucked out my phone, shaking it a little bit over the toilet. With my phone in her hand, she swerved around me and opened the cabinet under the bathroom sink where a small hand towel was stored, wrapping my phone in it.

A simple smile pinned to her face, she stretched her hand in my direction and said, "You're welcome. I don't have any rice or whatever to help you out...but you're still welcome."

Well, there went the rice idea.

Taking the towel with the phone, I pressed the power button, and as expected, the screen did absolutely nothing.

When the barista saw my irritation, I tried to press out the most genuine grin I could. "Thank you."

Then the loudest damn gust of wind I'd ever heard slammed into the front of the shop, the windows trembling and the light bulbs dangling above us swinging gently side to side.

"Um...maybe it will slow down soon. I don't think those travel bans last very long." Her words had a hint of uncertainty to them—maybe even a little fear.

Another gust of wind slammed into the door just as a phone beeped from the counter.

Well, we knew that wasn't *my* phone.

Fuck, how was I going to get to Merlin Heights tonight?

Kati would now feel as if I ghosted her on our first date.

She'd probably be at the restaurant in one hour in some sleek, red dress—not too fancy, but not too casual—with her dark hair pinned back out of her eyes. She'd tap her foot a few times and look around, probably only waiting fifteen minutes to leave and never respond to my messages whenever I could get back to her.

We'd only been texting for two weeks, and in my defense, I barely knew her.

But I knew her enough to know she'd be the perfect plus-one at my brother's wedding.

Well-spoken, attractive, polite.

Though I wanted Kati to be the only thing on my mind, now I had this woman in front of me to worry about on top of the anxiety I'd have at work tomorrow.

My phone was the keeper of my map, my contacts, my email, my organizer.

I felt completely naked.

The elven barista twisted on her heel and pushed some strands of blonde hair behind her *very* pierced ears before looking down at her phone. Pressing her lips together, she said, "I take that back...this is *another* travel ban notification telling us to stay off the roads. It's like they're threatening us...but trying to be nice about it."

"Dammit," I whispered under my breath, taking the glasses off my face again and pinching the bridge of my nose. "Fuck."

"Is it really *that* bad that you have to stay in here for a little while longer? You could be stranded in your car in the middle of nowhere, you know," she said, sass clinging to every word. It was sass, but the kind of sass you couldn't take seriously. It was too high pitched and kind to sound brash. Honestly, it was kind of cute how tough she was trying to sound. "At least you have coffee, and leftover pastries, and a fire, and blank—"

"Am I complaining?" I asked, facing her as she leaned against the wooden counter. "I...I'm not complaining. I just...I have a date in an hour."

Her shoulders slumped for a second, and as if she could tell her body had reacted to my statement, she perked her body back into a healthy posture. "Body language speaks volumes, Langston. You were complaining."

"It's Liam," I said softly, placing the glasses back on my face. I sat down on the chair behind me and finally let myself breathe. If I wasn't leaving anytime soon, I had to come to terms with the fact that I wouldn't see Kati tonight. I guess having a fireplace at my back and coffee only a few feet away would keep me calm in the meantime. I had no other choice. "And I'm not mad. I'm not mad at *you*, that is. I'm mad that my phone is out of commission, and I'm mad I'll be leaving this girl hanging. It's not what I do. And now I don't know how I'll get in touch with her, and I also have to reschedule tomorrow's meeting with—"

"Okay, I get it. Your head is going in every direction." She pushed herself up onto the wooden counter, sitting cross-legged beside the tablet that played the part as register. I guessed when you owned the place, you could sit wherever you wanted...even on a counter. With your *bare* feet crossed beneath you. When had she even taken her shoes off? "It's not *me* you're mad at...it's Mother Nature."

"Yes! Exactly." I threw my hands into the air before looking back toward the front windows.

White.

All I saw was white.

All I heard was the howling wind.

Fuck you, Mother Nature.

"Al."

I turned back toward the cross-legged barista and heavily sighed. "No...it's Liam."

She giggled, throwing her head back so cropped, blonde hair fell over her face. When her eyes met mine again, she said, "I know *your* name is Liam. Me. I'm Alice...or Al. Whichever. I went a little crazy with your name and forgot to tell you mine."

"Oh," I said, clearing my throat before unbuttoning my sleeve cuffs. If I wasn't going anywhere, I might as well get comfortable, which was incredibly hard to do in this getup. "Okay. Thanks for letting me know."

Yeah, at this point, I really couldn't get any more uncomfortable.

My *awkward* was showing.

"Were you all dressed up for this date of yours? Or do you dress like this every day?" Alice asked, circling her index finger in the air to outline my body.

"I came from a meeting and decided it was close enough to the restaurant's attire. So...I just kept it on."

"What do you do?"

"I run a production company."

"Where?"

"Kind of all over the place...the main office is in Rockberry." I coughed into my fist, adjusting my tie. "Why are you grilling me?"

She shrugged, sliding her thumb casually across her phone and clicking on the screen. Tease. "You could be a murderer. I'm just trying to decide whether or not you are one."

Laughing, my tie finally loosened, and I slipped it off, eyeing it before looking at Alice over my glasses. "Do you think I'm going to use this *fancy* tie to strangle you right here in your own café? Maybe I'll chop your body up and feed it to customers?"

Her eyes widened—which was surprising because her eyes were already the size of saucers—and her throat shifted as she lowered her phone and said, "See...right there. I don't know you well enough to know if you're being serious or sarca—"

"Sarcasm." I balled the tie up and tossed it onto the fleece blanket folded atop the walnut table. "I'm being 100% sarcastic. Can't you tell?"

She lifted one brow just as the lights flickered, both of our necks snapping upward to watch the golden glow fade and return. "After hearing how angry you sounded in the bathroom and then how angry you were about having to stay here for a while…you could be a ginger barbarian with anger issues who I should stay far, far away from."

"I'm the only one who can call myself a ginger barbarian," I said monotonously, trying not to laugh. "And barbarians have full beards. I do not."

For being a spunky little sprite, she was entertaining, to say the least.

The lights flickered again just as Alice's bare feet quickly found the floor, and she wandered behind me to the fireplace still roaring with heat.

"So…do you use a laptop or anything when you're working? Do you have, like, an office hidden in the back?" I asked, facing Alice as she stood with her back to the flames.

Snickering, she said, "Why, yes. If you go behind the counter and pull a lever, it will lower you down into my underground lair where you can find every piece of technology ever created. I'm in the process of making robot baristas, actually, since my part-time employees keep calling out last minute."

I just stared at her, expressionless.

I knew she'd be the first to break, her giggle echoing through the room before she said, "Sarcasm. See…I can do it too."

"Uh-huh." My face barely shifted.

"Okay, okay. I don't have an *office*, but my laptop is at my place in the back." Alice lifted her chin in the direction of a door that looked painted into the wall, hidden in the forest of tapestries and watercolors.

Following her gaze, I said, "Your place is…"

"Attached to the café? Yeah. Just like in Merlin Heights, every building here is attached to another one in some way." Alice took a step away from the fire before hesitating and slowly twisting on her heel to face me. "If this is a way to lure me into a more secluded area to murder me, just know that I already texted my best friend, and she knows I'm with some big burly giant named Liam who does production things."

I wasn't surprised that was who she'd been texting.

If anything, I was impressed. She was being cautious, and I respected that.

"I'm not going to murder you. If it makes you feel any better, I will stay three feet away from you at all times," I said, getting to my feet and dangling the tie around my neck. "I just wouldn't mind emailing my co-workers to give them an update and messaging Kati through the My Cup app. No one knows that my entire life was just at the bottom of your toilet."

Alice's dark eyes looked me up and down, but not without a cautious squint to them. Taking two quick steps toward the back corner of the café, she said, "Three feet. You can use my laptop."

"Thank you," I responded, trying to sound as genuine as I could since this woman had some obvious trust issues she had to work out. As I walked by the counter, I stopped at my phone that sat on the damp washcloth. Pressing and holding the power button again, I waited.

Nothing.

Before we got to the door, her ringed hand on the handle, she whispered, "And if you come any closer, Archibald will pounce on you, claw your eyes out, and eat them for dinner."

"What the fuck is an Archibald?" I asked.

Smiling, she twisted the handle and opened the door. "You'll see."

CHAPTER THREE

Alice

WHAT THE FUCK WAS I thinking?

I was letting a complete stranger into my home in the middle of a snowstorm when it would take hours for someone to come to my rescue, and, by then, I'd probably be chopped up into twelve different pieces.

I was cool.

I was collected.

I thrived off being cool and collected.

Or thinking I was, at least.

"You can log on over there." Once Liam closed the door and we both stood in my studio, I gestured toward the small desk opposite my bed, overlooking what, usually, was Holly Hill Ski Resort. Gems and stones and trinkets lined the desk, surrounding a small corkboard leaning against the window. Behind the corkboard, all you could see was white.

The whitest of whites.

"I get why you live here," Liam said, absorbing the small space. I could tell he, too, was looking out all the windows—either because he could barely see out of them or because the entire space was practically made of them.

"It's not much, but it's just enough," I said with a shrug, slipping my feet into the moccasin-style slippers beneath my bed. "My dad and uncle used to do a lot with real estate in the Finger Lakes area. This was once another storefront, but he made it into a ground loft, of sorts, when I took over the coffee shop."

"*Took over*," Liam repeated, sitting down in the swivel chair by my desk, his large body looming over the laptop as he clicked it to life. "Did someone else own it before?"

"My mom did, yeah," I murmured, getting down onto my knees and looking beneath the bed. Smiling, I reached far underneath. "Oh, there you are!"

"Was the coffee shop a family place?"

"Yes."

"Did you always—"

"No. Now, is it *your* turn to grill *me*?" I snapped, twisting onto my side beneath the bed until I finally hugged Archibald's golden, furry body. "Oh, come on!"

"Well...fair is fair," Liam mumbled, clicking on the laptop until a heavy sigh sounded...similar to the one coming from me when Archibald slipped from my grip with a hiss. "Aaaand your laptop is updating."

"Oh, that means we have a solid fifteen minutes until you can try logging on again." There was a hint of annoyance clinging to every word as I slid out from the underside of my bed—catless.

Liam threw his arms into the air. "What? Why is everything taking so long around here?"

"What else is taking a long time, *Larson*?" I asked coldly, hoping my personality would warm back up in the coming minutes.

A few seconds of silence passed.

"The storm...it's taking a long time for the storm to pass."

"If that's all you got, then you shouldn't complain." I was starting to get annoyed at the guy—well, maybe not entirely at *him*, but at the scene at hand.

A stranger was whining in my studio.

Archibald was being a dick.

I couldn't leave my place even if I wanted to.

But, then again, I knew I *wouldn't* leave.

Liam twisted in the swivel chair, his long legs shifting back and forth. "So, what are all these postcards?"

"Do you mean the pictures?" I asked, leaning against the bed, defeated.

"Well, aren't these all just the pictures on the backs of postcards?"

I knew exactly what he was looking at. Nine or ten postcards were pinned to the corkboard in front of him, showcasing beautiful beaches and mountains and islands. Whenever a friend went on a vacation over the last few years—most of these were from Dana—I asked them to bring back a postcard for me. As 1990s as it seemed to collect them, I liked looking at the gorgeous landscapes and resorts and places I knew I'd never get to visit.

It was the most relaxing tease.

"They're just places I'll never get to," I explained nonchalantly. "I like collecting them and daydreaming. I'm guessing you visit lots of fancy places in your line of work…I'm just guessing that's what producers do."

"I mean, I do travel. A lot," Liam said, turning back toward the laptop. "*Too* much."

"How could you travel *too* much? You get to constantly refresh and rejuvenate in new places."

"Why will you never visit these places?" he asked, redirecting.

I reached back under the bed, not sure exactly what I was reaching for at this point, since Archibald was being an asshole. "I have Snowcap to run. I can't just leave."

"But…you can. You can always take time off for—"

"No," I exclaimed, my response quicker and firmer than I meant it to sound. Taking a deep breath, I placed my friendly, barista façade back on my face. "No, I mean…I just can't take time off. I have to run the place for my parents."

"Are they on va—"

"Let's play a game," I spat.

"What?"

"A card game. Let's do something to pass the time," I said, finding a rectangular box beneath my bed. Pulling it out, I set it on the floor between us. "Soooo…*cards* it is!"

Liam adjusted his glasses, leaning toward the box. "That's not a card game."

"It's *Share or Scare*."

"Is it a children's game?"

"Absolutely not!" Jaw dropped, I hugged the box to my chest. "You just wait until you hear some of these questions. *Then* you'll realize it's not a children's game. Do you want wine?"

"Yes," he said quickly, looking over his shoulder to check the status of the update.

23% complete.

Making my way to the nook by the door that housed the world's tiniest stovetop and minifridge, I took out the bottle of rosé I'd opened a few days before, when snow had, yet again, caused chaos in Holly Hill. Pouring us each a glass, I handed one off to Liam, who nodded in thanks as I returned to my spot on the floor, crossing my legs.

"We're playing this on the floor like it's a middle school sleepover?" Liam asked, getting to his feet. Now he *really* was looming over me.

"How do you know what girls do at middle school sleepovers?"

"I have two older sisters and a little brother. I overheard my sisters a *lot* because they thought their squeals were whispers." To my surprise, Liam lowered himself to the hardwood floor, morphing his body into a version of the cross-legged position I sat in. His version just looked a little more painful than mine did.

I mean, he had to be twenty feet tall, wearing a suit, and sitting on the hard, cold floor.

That in itself *sounded* painful.

"Are you guys all close?" I asked, tapping my fingers atop the box.

Liam shrugged, nodding. "Yeah, I'd say we are. My brother and I have always been close. Hell, people thought we were twins for the longest time. He's a lawyer in Rockberry and is getting married this spring to a first-grade teacher. They have a golden retriever and a big brick house with a white picket fence and all that shit."

His voice trailed off.

"It sounds like you either look up to him—pun intended—or you think he's living a bit too *perfect* of a life."

"Well...both," Liam muttered, running fingers through his auburn hair. "I love the guy. Even though he's younger, I've always seen him as a role model. He was also *really* excited about this date for me. Not that I'm not proud of my line of work—I am—but his excitement for me to finally date again and get married keeps making me question all this traveling I do."

Well, at least he *could* travel.

And get dates.

All my dates drove or flew away the next day to some bigger, *better* city.

I wasn't sure how to respond to this whole *missing his date* debacle—nor did I want to. I also didn't *really* want to get any closer to this guy than need be because: 1) he'd be gone in the morning, 2) he was looking forward to meeting this Kati character, and 3) he was annoyingly good looking.

Red flag, red flag, red flag.

Instead of pestering him more about his relationship with his brother or his excitement for this date, it seemed like a good time to redirect.

"Okay. So...*Share or Scare*. You really want to play?" I asked, opening the top of the cardboard box to reveal a line of cards—half of them red and the other half orange.

"I already got down on the floor, and we have"—Liam looked over his shoulder at the laptop—"another 60% until the damn thing finishes updating."

Smiling against the lip of my wine glass, I took a sip. "So, this game is kind of like the adult version of *Truth or Dare*...but I *promise* it won't become one of *those* kinds of games. I mean...you're a stranger."

"A stranger you let walk right into your home." Liam's eyebrow lifted as he took a sip of rosé. "Does it often become one of *those* games?"

I swallowed slowly, my chest surprisingly growing warm. "No! No. Not really. How about we give each other five free passes on cards we find inappropriate. We can keep the questions on a friendly...or *customer*...level."

"What's the share, and what's the scare?" he asked directly, setting the wine down and unbuttoning his jacket. Looking away from his fingers as they plucked each button free, I took a long gulp of wine as his deep-blue jacket hit the floor.

He was wearing a white button-up beneath the jacket, Alice.

He wasn't trying to insinuate a damn thing.

So, why was my brain insinuating?

He would be gone tomorrow, like all the rest.

"The orange cards are share cards...kind of like truth, but they're usually deeper, or more nostalgic, or a little—I don't know—*friskier* than just a typical truth."

Liam nodded, taking another sip.

"The red cards are scare cards," I said, looking up to meet his gaze. Light eyes connected with mine, and I blinked a couple times before saying, "These cards want you to do something that may *scare* the other person, but it can be in a playful, or goofy, or...frisky way."

"You like that word."

"What word?"

"Frisky," Liam said, a low laugh sounding in his chest. "You've said it twice."

"Well, it's a great descriptor for some of the cards in here, *Lawrence*."

Laughing that same, chesty laugh again, he said, "Okay. And I'm guessing we roll the dice, and it tells us which card to pick. Yes?"

"It sure does." I grabbed the dice and tossed it in the air, grinning when I caught it perfectly. "And it looks like you're going first."

"Why do I have to go first?" Liam asked, looking back over his shoulder at the laptop.

53% left.

"Because it says whoever cried last goes first, and since you've been whining a lot, we're going to count that." I opened the teeny instruction packet so it was almost directly in Liam's face, a smile unfolding across my own. "Let's play."

CHAPTER FOUR

Liam

I WAS ABOUT TO play a non-children's game in an angsty pixie's first-floor *loft*...that was pretty badass, in all honesty.

As cliché as it sounded, it felt like we were sitting at the center of a snow globe—the walls almost all glass with curtains still pulled back so white was all we saw. It was obvious the space was once a boutique or another coffee shop or something along those lines, but the transformation making it a livable space was pretty fantastic.

Feeling completely closed in with this small woman—while still phone-less—shouldn't have given me the sense of comfort I felt as I sat on this floor.

Was I annoyed the laptop was taking seven years to update? Sure was.

Was I mad I didn't have a working phone? Absolutely.

Did I finally want to meet up with Kati? Yeah.

But did I want to leave the second I finished typing out a few emails and messages? I didn't.

Adjusting my glasses, I rolled the dice and read the first card—which was orange. "*What is a childhood memory you will never forget?*"

"See! That's a pretty calm one, don't you think?" Alice said, throwing her hands into the air, silver bangles clinking at her wrists.

"They get less calm?" I asked.

Alice leaned forward, a little blonde braid at the front of her face falling over her eyes as she poked the top of the card. "That little sunshine symbol means its calm. The raindrop goes into some deeper topics, and the flame is...well, you can guess."

"I can't guess, Alice. You have to tell me." I lifted an eyebrow. Her expression didn't falter, which impressed me.

"Tell me a childhood memory, Lenny."

I leaned back onto my hands. "I used to have skinny dipping parties in my parents' pool in high school."

"*That's* your *greatest* core memory?" Alice asked, her pink pout twisting. "What about when you were, like, actually a child...not a teen?"

"I used to skinny dip a lot as a kid and get in trouble for it."

"I sense a *really* weird theme." Her gaze raked up and down my body. "I don't see you as the skinny-dipping type. You're too...too put-together for that."

"Well, the suit is a good act," I said, handing her the card. Her hands didn't budge as she looked down at it. "I was the wild card of the family—pun intended."

"Clever."

"Thanks," I laughed, loosening my belt just the tiniest bit so I could breathe while sitting on this damn floor. "My little brother was the perfect student and athlete, and my sisters were both theater nerds who stayed at musical practice until nine every night. Someone had to shake things up a little bit."

Alice nodded, biting her bottom lip. "I wonder if you'll showcase any of this wild side you speak of."

I loosened my belt a little more, this time her eyes darting to my hands as they moved. "Your turn."

"Huh?" Alice asked, her body leaning away from mine.

"It's your turn to tell me about your greatest childhood memory."

"I don't have to answer it. That was *your* card." Her voice was hushed, almost a little hoarse. Typically, I'd push the matter, just to be a dick, but it didn't feel right pressing her to spill secrets from her childhood if she didn't want to. Her eyes darkened when the question hit her, giving me pause. Maybe this snowstorm and buzzed barista were making me soft.

I pushed people.

It was part of my job.

I pushed until I got my way—at least in the world of television, I did.

Alice grabbed the wine bottle from her side table and poured herself another glass, gesturing in my direction as I nodded, and she poured me some more. After taking a hefty sip, she licked her lips and smiled. It was her *barista smile*—the one that almost looked trained. Practiced. Perfected.

"My turn," she said with a slight shimmy, rolling the dice and reaching into the box. Her eyes grew even larger—something I didn't think possible—when she chose a red card with a flame at the top of it.

"This may be interesting," I whispered, taking a long, *long* sip.

Alice brought her finger to the tip of her nose and tapped it, as if it helped her think. "Huh. Okay."

"Okay."

"Alright," she said, tapping her nose two more times before biting her lip and looking me dead in the eye. "Take your shirt off."

Well, that was unexpected.

"Wha...what?" I stammered, looking down at my button-up and loosened tie.

She pushed her chin out in my direction. "I can tell you're uncomfortable in your fancy little outfit. Take the shirt off."

"What the hell did that card say?" I asked, shaken. Alice straightened her arm so I could see her card: *Tell someone to take something off.*

Well.

She followed those directions pretty damn well.

My eyes never left hers as I brought the wine glass to my lips before setting it back on the floor. When I reached toward my buttons—trying far too hard to look *cool*, my hands almost hit my glass. I expected her to look away, blush a little bit, and maybe fidget as I took these damn layers off. Her eyes had wandered a little bit before, but once she'd demanded I remove my shirt, her eyes were all on me.

She didn't break our eye contact.

Not even the slightest bit.

Those dark eyes were lasered to mine.

My fingers brushed the button of my shirt, unbuttoning it before moving on to the next. My shirt fell open, falling over my shoulders and down my arms until I added it to the pile at my waist. As I took my glasses off, I noticed the tip of her finger fall between her lips—either she was biting at a hangnail, or her head was spinning in ways my body was already reacting to.

If she continued pouring these glasses of wine and looking at me with those eyes of hers, I was going to rip through my pants before getting the chance to take them off.

They were growing tighter by the second.

So much for comfort.

"So, did I *scare* you?" she asked, removing her finger from between her teeth.

"Huh? Yeah. I guess you can say that," I responded, adjusting my belt again before reaching for the dice. As I went to roll it, I heard another giggle whisper from her. Looking up, I asked, "Why...what's so funny?"

Alice brought the tip of her index finger back to her mouth, giggling against it before she said, "You're pierced."

I looked down at my chest, and two metal barbells came into view. "Um...yes. Yup, I am."

"I just didn't see that coming," she whispered, her voice almost lost in the howl of the wind hitting the windows. "You're just so—"

"*Put together*?" I raised an eyebrow as I set my glasses back on the bridge of my nose. "Don't judge a book by its cover, Alice. The cliché stands true."

The dice told me to pick an orange card, and as I looked down at the raindrop symbol and scanned the words, I peered up to see Alice wipe her lips on the back of her hand. Bouncing my gaze from her to the card and back to her again, I wasn't sure how this question was going to play out after her quick reaction earlier.

But this was part of the game.

And the game must go on.

"*What's the first word that comes to mind when I say* family."

The air stilled, and Alice sat there like a statue made of marble—cross-legged with her wine glass in hand. For a moment, I thought I needed to repeat myself, but I could tell she'd heard every word as clear as the flickering lights above us.

Bringing the wine to her lips, she quickly finished off the glass and set it aside. "Gone."

CHAPTER FIVE

Alice

Well, I hadn't expected the night to go this way.

I thought maybe we'd have a few drinks, play the silly game, and if I was lucky, get a good snuggle session in.

I mean, the guy was handsome as hell.

I kind of wanted to climb him like a fucking black diamond ski slope.

But I also knew he was very set on going on this date of his. Plus, this guy was like all the rest—he would leave once the snow began to calm down. He'd head to Merlin in no time, apologizing to Kati, and figuring out whatever next steps he needed to take with his big, bad production company. He'd forget cuddling up with a flaky barista in the middle of nowhere within twenty-four hours.

I'd go back to being alone.

I wasn't one to think this negatively. I'd become very good at replacing those sulking thoughts with ones of hope and holiday cheer. I'd focus on the energy in the air during this time of year instead of the negativity clouding my mind.

A hot mug of coffee warming cold hands.

Being cocooned in a favorite fleece blanket.

Children smiling.

Couples holding hands.

Families laughing.

Dammit.

That wasn't where I meant for my mind to go.

I adjusted my seat on the floor and looked Liam's way again when I went for my third refill of the night. I was feeling a little warm and gooey and knew one more should be my last. He nodded, and I poured him a hefty glass before he went back to staring at me through those dark-rimmed glasses that fit his face far too well.

"Gone..." he whispered into his glass. "I'm..."

"Please don't say you're sorry," I said, flapping my hand in his direction—the metal clinking at my wrists making me jump. "They've been gone three years. It's okay. It's fine."

The wine met my lips.

His eyes stayed lasered to mine.

I knew his next question.

"Car crash. Right outside the shop." I angled my head toward the door we'd come in through thirty minutes before. "It was a slippery night. Kind of...kind of like tonight."

Liam's mouth fell slightly open before his lips closed back together.

I knew he wanted to say sorry.

I knew he wanted to ask me how I was.

He probably wanted to hug me close, my head against his soft chest and mere inches from his nipple piercings I couldn't stop staring at.

My mind was thinking about nipple piercings while his was quite obviously in a state of mourning.

Maybe I *was* numb to it all.

"*I'll* be the one to say sorry. I put a damper on all this," I said with a laugh, circling my hand in the air above the box of cards.

"No damper. You answered the question honestly," Liam said, setting down his wine. "Though I'm impressed you didn't break when you answered that, it's also okay if you do. You can. You probably should."

"That's a lot of work...breaking down," I stated, scooting the box closer. "It takes a lot of energy, and I'd rather use that energy elsewhere. Like...playing this game. It's my turn."

"Alice." His voice was low and soft, his head hanging to the side. "Are you okay?"

If I had a penny for every time someone asked me that.

I sat up straighter, reaching into the box of cards. "I am. Yes. Thank you for asking, Leonard."

Of course I'd pick a share card.

"Okay...huh. Wow," I said, cheeks flushing as I read the card for a second time. "*Have another player tell the person holding this card what they find fascinating about them.*"

Were my cheeks hot because of the wine?

I was absolutely blaming the wine.

"*Fascinating*, huh? It's fascinating how that question turned back on me," Liam whispered, his lips pinching into a curious grin. "But fascinating. That's an interesting word to work with."

"Remember, you can always take a pass. We have—"

"I'm not taking a pass." The certainty in his voice was deafening. He took a sip of wine, brows furrowed in concentration, swallowed, and said, "I find you fascinating because you come across as this bright ray of sunshine, dancing through your coffee shop, waiting to be whisked away on Santa's sleigh."

I mean, he wasn't wrong.

I was kind of waiting to be someone's Mrs. Claus.

Santa could come scoop me up at any time.

But would I actually get on that sleigh if I had the chance?

"But what's fascinating is your ability to mask some darkness inside of you. You feel it's necessary to be a bright light to the world around you rather than sit with that darkness. It's fascinating—maybe not the healthiest—but your light is definitely one we all can see...and appreciate."

"Are you *really* a therapist or something? That, or you're an author."

"I'll take that as a compliment." Liam brought the wine to his lips, shimmying his shoulders a little bit as he snickered against the glass. "I'm a professional serial killer. Remember?"

My stomach dropped. "Not funny. You still could be."

Liam wiped his lips on the back of his hand. "All I said was true, though. I hope you can see how you brighten up the world just by being in it."

He seemed to catch himself after saying the last sentence, blinking a few times before he stated, "Well, like...how you're so friendly and energetic when taking customers' orders. I'd been on the phone when I placed my order with you, but you still smiled and were all peppy and shit."

"Which is surprising because I hate when people are on the phone when I take their order." Fury instantly rolled through me. "I'm surprised I didn't *accidentally* charge you a little extra. It may or may not have happened before."

"I wouldn't have noticed." His eyes met mine, and I realized how green they were. Deep and emerald and almost tie-dye, a mix of hazel spiraling at the center. "But I noticed *you*."

I didn't believe him.

If he had, he would have come back to get his damn dirty chai.

"Your turn," I said, sitting up straight and nudging the cards toward him. "And don't pick a—"

"It's a scare."

"Dammit, why are the scares and shares rotating like this?" I asked, shaking my head.

"Because we're stuck in a snowstorm, your laptop is *still* updating, and the universe knows we need entertainment." Laughing, Liam lifted the card so it covered his face. He peeked around the card before hiding behind it again. "Are you ready?"

"It can't be *that* intense, Lucky."

"*That* nickname is pushing it."

I shrugged. "I'm running out of name fuel. What's the question? Lay it on me."

"That's kind of what it says."

Crinkling my brow, I asked, "*What* does it say?"

"It...it wants me to lay it on you."

For a moment, I had zero idea what the fuck he wanted to lay on me. But when Liam set the card down and leaned forward, morphing into a crawling position so he was mere inches away from me, I realized exactly what it meant.

"Three...three feet. Remember?" I whispered as he crawled closer, forcing me back onto my forearms. He was so close, his heat warming my already buzzing body. The buzz—the thrill—was intoxicating as he hovered above me.

"Is that really what you want? Three feet?" he asked softly, his voice falling back into that hushed, low tone I could listen to all night—I *wanted* to listen to all night.

This was it.

This was the moment he'd forget about in twenty-four hours once he left Holly Hill and met Kati.

This was when I had to push aside any weird emotions stirring inside of me—that *had* to be from the wine—because this man wasn't anything but a stranger.

But this also was a moment I did not—could not—push aside.

Because, dammit, I wanted to feel something. Anything. Before that, too, was taken from me.

"No. I don't," I whispered, my head finding the floor as I lay flat beneath him. "I don't want three feet between us."

Liam looked down at me, his head slowly cocking to the side. "Tell me what you *do* want, Alice."

The wind howled.

The lights flickered.

The door handle shook.

But all I felt was his body on mine as he lowered himself on top of me, his hand reaching below my head to string his fingers through my hair. He tipped my head back the slightest bit, and my lips fell open, tasting his breath on mine.

"I want you to kiss me, Liam."

CHAPTER SIX

Liam

THE SECOND MY NAME dripped from her lips, I was done.

I lost the control I'd zipped up tight inside of me—and I'd zipped up a *lot* of willpower in the last hour.

When Alice began talking about her parents, I'd wanted to fling myself across our more than three-foot separation and hold her close. I'd wanted to kiss her forehead and stroke her golden hair. I'd wanted to tip her chin up so her eyes fell into mine.

This woman.

In the last hour alone, she'd made me soft, made me open up, and made me crave more of her flighty positivity.

Even when she let that mask fall.

My lips didn't just caress hers. They pressed with certainty, hunger. My fingers threaded and gently pulled at her blonde hair, the sweetest gasp escaping her lips—lips I could tell were upturned into a grin. Her smile against my mouth felt so damn good—*tasted* so good—I needed more.

"Do you still want three feet?" I whispered, my lips trailing from her soft neck to the skin behind her ear. Her scent was a mix of peppermint and something sugar sweet, and I wanted to fully consume it.

Consume *her*.

"No. This...this right here is good. It's *really* good." Her voice was strained but not without an ounce of energy to it. Eagerness. Pep. I didn't even know it was possible to sound like you were pulling back while also going full throttle.

"I'm glad you think so." I gently pulled her earlobe between my teeth, one hand caressing her cheek before wandering to her throat, stopping right above the slight line of cleavage peeking out from the oversized, cropped sweater falling off her shoulders. "Do you want to keep playing this game, Alice?"

Her eyes widened in thought as she darted her gaze toward the box behind me. "Slide the box over."

"*Really*?" I whined, kissing her from her earlobe to her throat, tipping her head back so her lips parted the tiniest bit.

"Really," she responded breathily. "Grab a red card."

"That's cheating, missy." I continued kissing her neck, licking a line from the underside of her chin to her lips. She shuddered, and I pressed my forehead against hers covered in wispy, blonde strands.

"If you *really* want some entertainment tonight, you *will* grab a red card." The certainty in her little voice immediately caused my dress pants to grow tighter as I pressed down against her, rolling my hips.

Just as I felt her body react to my movements, I backed away, reaching for a card. Releasing my grip from her mess of hair was devastating, but if she wanted to truly stay occupied during this snowstorm—and she wanted to do this with *me*—I would not say no.

I mean, I probably *should* have said no.

I needed to check the laptop and reschedule my date with Kati.

Instead, Alice was forcing all those thoughts into the storm, the wind whisking them away at warped speed.

"It's your turn." Without looking at the card, I handed it over to her as she lay beneath me.

Her lips scrunched to the side of her face as she read it, her nose crunching before our eyes met. "Sit up."

Again with that voice. The gruffness to it was such a shock to my system, coming from this petite thing. Her tone was one you couldn't say no to, making me wonder if she even knew she held this power. As requested, I sat back before realizing I needed to loosen my belt a little more if I was going to make it at least another ten minutes.

And that was pushing it.

With my knees up and separated—my belt a bit looser and my cock a bit harder—I watched as *she* got onto *her* hands and knees this time. A tiny braid circled her face and hung in front of her large, deep eyes as she grew closer. When she rose up onto her knees, I could almost see up her baggy sweater as she towered above me.

Well, *towered* was a bit of an overstatement.

Before I could adjust my glance, pressure flew through her hand and forced me flat onto my back. "Your pants need to go."

"First my shirt and then my—"

"Do it, Louis."

With a lifted brow, I said, "That was a good one."

"Thanks." If it was possible to curtsy while on your knees, she'd perfected it. "Now do it."

I wasn't used to being bossed around. I bossed people around—I was *good* at it. This wasn't even some game of domination she was playing. It was more like the other side of her personality shining through. She was letting the darker, fiercer side overtake the bright, spirited body she lived in.

Even though I wasn't the one making this personality flip happen—the game was—I could tell it was necessary for her to bring it to life.

We all had part of ourselves hiding beneath the surface.

Sometimes it took one weird-ass night to bring it to light.

I lay flat on my back, the hardwood floors feeling warmer than they should on a night like this. Looking beneath the rims of my glasses, I watched her hands run through her hair before her head fell back with a giggle. When she looked down at me, her lips were twisted in the cutest, most playful—and devilish—grin I'd ever seen. The smile paired well with her ringed fingers that now fumbled at my belt buckle, that same giggle sounding as she finally unbuckled my pants and freed the button.

Fuck, I could finally breathe.

"Let's see here," she whispered, biting her bottom lip. Lifting my hips up a little to help her lower my pants, she pulled them all the way to my ankles and yanked them off over my red-and-green polka-dotted socks. Throwing the pants in the pile growing beside us, she said, "Red."

My brow furrowed. "Huh?"

Alice's gaze shifted away from my boxer briefs—briefs holding down one hell of a hard cock that was just as hard to ignore.

One I did *not* want her to ignore.

"Red," Alice repeated, reaching behind her and plucking the card off the floor by her wine glass. Twisting it so the words faced me, I squinted through my frames to read: *Find out the color of someone's underwear without asking.*

Again, she was very thorough with her process.

"Yup. They are red." I laughed, shaking my head against the ground. "Good work."

Alice set the card back with the others and peered over my shoulder at the laptop. "There's only 2% left to go for the update."

"Fuck the update," I said, placing my hands at her hips and pulling her on top of me. Immediately, she pressed her little body down right over my growing erection, her giggle not fooling me one bit.

She knew what she was doing to me.

I *liked* what she was doing to me.

The question was, how would this play out in the morning?

Would this be just a typical one-night stand—a one-night stand before I went on a *real* first date with someone who could possibly become something?

Something real? Something more?

Why did that make my stomach churn?

I didn't want to think about any of that. I didn't want to think about my stupid phone, or visiting my brother, or the dumb meetings I had lined up all day tomorrow. I didn't want to focus on the update because, now, my focus was elsewhere...and it was somewhere that felt really, really good. Not just physically, but mentally...emotionally. I felt oddly at ease inside this snow globe with Alice.

I really didn't want to escape it even though I knew, sooner or later, I'd have to.

Instead of awkwardly walking to the laptop, I ran my hands up her thighs—thighs covered in the thin fabric of her fringed skirt now pooling around my bare legs. Light pressure flowed through my fingers as I raked them up toward her hips, pressing my thumbs into the crease between her hips and sex. I could feel the outline of underwear beneath my touch, and holy shit, I'd never known something that subtle could make me want to fucking come on the spot, but it did.

The fact that I couldn't pull down whatever was under those clothes and taste her was the most beautiful torture.

"Should we pick—"

"Don't you dare say it, Alice," I grumbled, my hands wandering up the side of her body until her warm, silky skin lay beneath my touch. These cropped sweater things sure came in handy.

"You...you don't want to play? We can pick just *one* more card?"

Damn her and those ginormous puppy eyes.

How could someone not fall to their knees when she gave them that look?

I was about to get onto *my* knees in three seconds if she kept this look up.

"One..." I whispered, breathing out a heavy sigh. "I will pick *one* more card."

"But you're doing it because it's fun, right?" Her sentence came out surprisingly fast as I sat up to grab the box behind her. One of my hands fell to the small of her back to keep her balanced, similar to how I'd caught her in the bathroom a couple hours before. The déjà vu must have hit us both because as I reached into the box, our breathing faltered.

"Yes," I responded, plucking a card from the box with a grin she seemed to just paste onto my face. "It *is* fun."

"I knew you'd like it." She wiggled on top of me as I lay back flat on the floor. When she circled over my center, a knowing look in her eyes grew with every slight circle of her hips. I knew she could feel me below her, growing harder as each second passed.

My patience was wearing thin.

I needed to just get through this next card.

This *last* card.

"It's an orange one," I mumbled, taking my glasses off and setting them to the side. Squinting at the tiny, blurry words, I read: *If you could change one thing from the last five years, what would it be?*

It was as if her body deflated above mine, energy leaking out and floating into the air. Her eyes grew darker—a similar shade I'd seen a handful of minutes earlier, when we'd pulled a card that tugged at her heartstrings.

I could almost feel the pain I saw building behind those eyes.

"I'm starting to regret playing this game..." she mumbled, rolling her eyes and pasting on that familiar grin—the one I knew was only a façade. "Where are all the funny, feisty cards? Those are the ones I'm good at."

"You can use one of those passes you talked about," I said, pushing the box aside. "Or we can just stop playing."

"I thought you said this game was *fun*, Larry."

"You're deflecting, Allison."

She scrunched her nose and leaned away. "Ewww...don't do that ever again."

"Noted."

Still straddling my hips, I felt her weight shift as she took a deep breath, her eyes shutting for only a second before opening again. I wanted to mention to her that, again, this was only a game. She didn't need to share a damn thing with some stranger.

But then she began talking.

CHAPTER SEVEN

Alice

I OFFICIALLY REGRETTED PULLING out this stupid game.

If Archibald hadn't been so terrified to come out from under my bed, maybe we would have hyper-focused on that damn cat for an hour, and this game never would have happened.

I could have lied.

I could have made some silly story up.

But when your mind immediately jumped to *one* thought when a question like this was asked, you couldn't ignore it.

You had to open yourself up to the truth.

Even if that meant opening up to a stranger.

"If I could change one thing, it would be answering the phone." Even saying those words aloud were a stab to the gut—to the heart.

Liam brought one hand up beneath the back of his head, his brows furrowed. "Okay."

"Okay."

"Is that all?"

"Noooo..." I whined, my head falling back dramatically as I threw my hands up in defeat. "No...there's more to it than that."

"Okay...because I was a little confused if you meant just answering the phone in general or—"

"Answering my phone the night my parents died."

The words stung the back of my throat.

Bees attacked my vocal cords.

Cats clawed at my neck.

I felt everything around me shift as I slid off Liam, and he balanced on his elbows.

"I've never admitted this out loud before," I whispered, bringing my legs beneath me. "Damn, these cards can be therapeutic in really fucked-up ways."

"You don't have to share." Liam's hand flattened over my thigh, a gentle pressure radiating from it. "But we have all night, Alice. I'm a good listener."

I believed him.

I believed this beautiful stranger would sit here and listen to me spill my secrets. He'd listen to me share the grief I'd bottled up for years.

Even though I barely knew this man, I somehow knew it was okay to open up to him.

It felt natural...easy.

"The evening of my parents' car crash, they called me. They called me three times, actually." I took a long inhale, closing my eyes on the exhale. "It hadn't been snowing as bad as it is tonight, but it was icy, and the roads were, obviously, slick. I *hate* talking on the phone. I avoid it at *all* costs...even with family."

"I'm surprised. You seem like a phone talker." Liam smiled slyly as I rolled my eyes.

"I don't know what that insinuates, but anyway..." I said, reaching for my wine. "I didn't have backup at the shop, and I was super stressed. I sent my mom a quick text saying *Busy. Give me a few.* Five minutes later, there was a crash outside the shop doors."

Silence cracked through the pressure building in the air around us.

The last time I'd said these words aloud were to the police officers who came to the scene that night.

"The weather was bad. You can't—"

"What if they needed me? What if they needed me for something *so* badly that they'd been rushing? What if my mom opened my text when she was driving and looked down at it the moment they slid into the truck? What if—"

"Alice..." Warmth enveloped me as Liam's arms wrapped around my shaking body. I hadn't realized I'd started trembling until the heat of his body enclosed around mine. Then I breathed for, probably, the first time in five minutes. "You can't blame yourself. If anything, blame this damn weather, but don't blame yourself."

"But *I* texted them. *I* didn't answer their calls. I could have controlled this whole damn scene, and I didn't. I lost that control, and they lost their focus on the road," I said softly, leaning against the bed as he released my body, immediately making me miss the comfort. "I don't even know why they needed to talk to me so badly. I'll...I'll never know."

With so much spilling out of me, I could tell Liam was at a loss for words. He sat in front of me, looking far too handsome—I don't think I'd realized how attractive he was when I ran into him in the bathroom—just waiting. Listening. Letting me feel all the feels in this moment.

He didn't have to say a single word.

He just needed to be present.

That was enough.

"Want an espresso martini? Maybe some avocado toast?" I asked, my feet finding the floor. Standing up for the first time in minutes threw me into a vertigo haze from probably both the wine and my traumatic trip down memory lane. "There's a recipe a mixologist in Merlin Heights uses that I'm *obsessed* with, and, I mean, I make a mean avocado toast. Snowcap is known for it."

"Right...now?" Liam looked up at me and then toward the door leading back to the shop. "You *really* think you're in the mindset right now to add caffeine into the mix? And slimy veggie bread?"

My shoulders loosened, my arms hanging at my sides as I rolled my eyes. "Larry. *Slimy veggie* bread? And I'm around caffeine all day. It does nothing for me anymore but put me mentally at ease. This may be the *best* decision of the night."

Liam got to his feet. "I thought playing this game was."

Poking him in the chest, I stepped backward toward the door. "If it weren't for the game, we probably wouldn't be on our way to make martinis and toast at almost midnight during a snowstorm, would we?"

"I mean...we may have been. I still *really* don't know you all that well," Liam stated, following my lead. "Maybe this was your motive all along. Seduce me, drug my martini, and force me to eat slimy bread."

"See...*now* who's the paranoid one?" Twisting the door handle as wind slammed into my studio windows, I smiled. "Let the midnight caffeine rage begin."

*

After finding the recipe in my notes app (minus the one secret ingredient the mixologist wouldn't share on her site), I whipped up two near-perfect martinis. Dropping three beans atop the drinks, I started to think I should go to one of the workshops this mixologist in Merlin Heights held. Though I adored being a barista—creating caffeinated beauty was a passion—playing mixologist on the side could be something I dabbled in.

For now, I'd dabble with Liam.

There just wouldn't be any dabbling with the avocado toast—he'd been *very* clear with that.

As I handed him the drink, both of us clinking glasses together, I wondered again how long he would be around once the ban cleared. I pictured myself stepping into his shoes—or better yet, his *boats*—and traveling across the state, exploring new places and learning more about the Finger Lakes region. I wondered how freeing it felt, escaping some place after spending so much time feeling so...I don't know, *stuck*.

Maybe not stuck—that wasn't the right word.

I had to think of it as devoting myself to something that meant something.

Even if it meant staying put.

Forever.

"What's your next step, Lois?" I asked, taking a seat by the fire and wrapping a knit blanket around my legs. "I'm pretty sure the laptop finished its update."

He raised an eyebrow. "*Now* you're really pushing the name game."

"I'm going to start repeating L names, and I've been on a roll." I took a sip, the smoothness of the drink breathing life back into me after the last conversation drained some of it. "Don't make me repeat, please."

"I have no power in this discussion," Liam said with a grin.

"So, what is it?" I repeated.

Liam sat back in the chair next to me, taking a sip of his espresso martini. I could tell he was thinking about how magical this recipe was too. "Well, I...should probably go send some messages and emails after we finish these martinis. Right now, I look like a total asshole, ghosting Kati on our first date. Then I have to see my brother...and my family. We're doing the *early* Christmas thing before I head out to Rockberry and finalize the next show placement."

The way Liam looked down at his hands when he explained this was sullen—stressed, even. There wasn't excitement clinging to his words. He didn't discuss visiting family with the gusto someone who *had* a family should. He didn't show determination when it came to the placement of his next show.

For being such a big man, he looked pretty small.

"Do you...look forward to your family party?"

Liam nodded. "Yes. Yeah. It's always a lot of fun."

"What about the show placement?"

"What about it?"

I scooted to the edge of my chair. "Are you, like, looking forward to solidifying all the production things you do?"

"Yeah."

"You sound enthralled."

"You're grilling me, *Alicia*."

I rolled my eyes, slouching back in the chair and wrapping my legs tighter beneath the blanket. "You just don't sound very enthusiastic about seeing your family or doing the work things you do. I really don't understand what you do, so bear with me."

Liam sighed, leaning back into the chair so his bare chest was open toward the fire. I should have looked away, but there was no use fighting it. This view was decadent as he sat there in nothing but red boxer briefs and dark-rimmed glasses. "It's not that it isn't exciting or whatever. My family can be...a lot. They are all extroverts, and I'm...kind of an extroverted introvert, I guess. I'll talk to people and speak up—I mean, it's part of my job—but it exhausts me. I'd rather see my family in short spurts or go to meetings where it's one on one. But that's not the life I lead."

"What about your brother?" I asked.

"What about him?"

"You're close to him? Is he...I don't know, tiring too? Can you only take him in *spurts?*"

Liam twisted his lips to the side of his face. "With my brother...it's different. I feel like I don't get as exhausted around him, but I always act more *put together* around him than I actually am. I mean, he is more excited about this date than I am, because then I can finally settle down like he has. He's more excited about figuring out this next show's location than I am, because then I can catch my breath for a little while." Liam untwisted his lips, pushing out a faint grin. "Tonight's been a good change of pace. I've been able to catch my breath with you."

I ignored the butterflies lashing out in my belly.

Those feelings needed to be caged up.

"It's an honor," I said softly, looking back toward the fire. "So, if you could change one thing from the last five years, what would you change?"

Liam huffed out a laugh. "That was *your* question, not mine."

"Answer it," I demanded, peering at his glass. "Or you don't get a refill."

Liam rolled his eyes as he tried to suppress a chesty laugh. "In the last five years, huh?" He took a deep breath. "I'd put my feet down somewhere. I'd find myself a home."

"You don't have a home?"

Liam leaned over his knees, shaking his head. "I pretty much live in hotels and bed and breakfasts. My production company covers most stays, or we get solid discounts. So, I just live out of my suitcase...and the phone drying on your counter."

Alice looked over her shoulder toward the counter before saying, "It looks pretty dead."

"I don't see it coming back to life."

Facing me again, Alice softly said, "But that must...that must get a little lonely. Not having a community?"

Our eyes met, and my stomach spiraled. His eyes—as bright as they were—looked to be drowning in darkness. "It is. It's lonely."

"So, you'd probably change your pace. You'd slow down."

"Yeah...but do you think that kind of change happens easily?" Liam chuckled, finishing off his martini. "Change takes effort. It takes work. Sometimes it's easiest if you just keep riding the waves you're used to."

"Well, that's depressing as fuck," I whispered, shaking my head as the lights flickered above us. Once the lights seemed to go back to their usual glow, I looked toward Liam who was staring into the flames. "But I get it."

Liam nodded, facing me. "I think you do."

We grew silent as the fire crackled before us, snowy gusts slamming against the storefront windows. We would meet each other's eyes, push out a small, sideways grin, and go back to watching the fire as it performed for us.

Bringing the drink to my lips, I stared into the flames. "You know what else gets lonely?"

Liam nodded. "It probably gets lonely staying in one spot for a long time too."

Goosebumps crawled up my arms after he spoke the words. Looking at him, I held back the tears I hadn't expected to emerge after hearing him understand this as well as he seemed to. Maybe it wasn't that he understood it—maybe he felt it.

He could sense I felt trapped by guilt.

And all I could do was nod in response.

CHAPTER EIGHT

Liam

I HADN'T EXPECTED THIS night to turn into a trauma dump.

But, alas, here we were, two people sitting in front of a fire with empty martini glasses, talking about their pasts.

One of us wanted to slow down.

The other wanted to see more. Do more. *Be* more.

For two people with such heavy thoughts, we couldn't have had more different end games.

That was what brought me back to the present—back to the reason I'd asked to go into her studio in the first place. "Maybe I should go check the My Cup app...and my email."

Alice's head snapped toward me, her brow furrowed. "Oh. Yeah...you probably should."

I paused before lifting my glass in the air a little bit more. "You said a refill was an option?"

"I thought you were afraid I was going to drug you? You're going to start wobbling soon enough if you keep up with this pace." Her laugh seemed almost forced as she got to her feet, placing a hand on her hip.

"You're the size of one of Santa's elves, Alice," I said as I got to my feet as well and stepped toward her. "*You're* the one who is going to be *wobbling*."

Alice's jaw dropped, and her hand flew to her chest dramatically. "Sir, Santa's elves drink spiked hot cocoa regularly. Our livers are *very* used to this, thank you very much."

I took another step toward her, forgetting for a moment that I was standing there in only my boxer briefs and socks. She didn't step back, just stood there with her martini glass in hand. "Is a refill still on the table, Alice?"

Our eyes locked, and after a few seconds, she rolled her eyes, snatching the glass from my hand. "Yeah, yeah. It is. We each get one more of these before we go to sleep and—"Again, she paused.

Sleep.

Sooner or later, we'd have to figure out sleeping arrangements since it was *very* obvious this snow wasn't slowing down anytime soon.

This reminded me, yet again, that I needed to get on her laptop as soon as possible.

I needed to move forward in some capacity before the night ended and morning smacked us both in the face.

"We…we'll figure that out after this last drink," I said, stepping around her toward the door to her studio. "Should I worry about Archibald?"

"Yes," she said confidently, wandering behind the counter. "You definitely should. He doesn't like strange men talking to other women in my bedroom."

Well, that verbiage was unexpected.

And kind of an odd punch in the gut.

"You think I'm still some *strange* man? I mean…I did just spill some of my guts out to you about my family and all that," I stated, pausing with my hand around the door handle. "If you feel uncomfortable with me messaging Kati, I can—"

"No…no, no, no." Alice flapped her hand in my direction as she shook her head. Keeping her focus on the drinks in front of her, she said, "I'm fine. You should check in with her. She deserves a date with you. She's a lucky girl."

My hand didn't shift on the handle, and my eyes didn't leave Alice as her back faced me, and she continued to putter behind the counter.

"She seems like someone who could slow down life with you—someone in a town you can work from and stay busy in while also making it a home." She continued to babble, mixing the martinis. "I'm sure she's tall and smart and would love to travel with you when you need to travel. You should check in with her…*really*."

I didn't move.

She was very good at being passive aggressive.

For a moment, I thought about twisting the handle and walking into her studio to dive into all the inboxes I had to check. For a moment, I wanted to walk away from this beautiful woman who'd poured out her heart to me minutes before.

For a moment, I thought about leaving.

Instead, I turned on my heels and walked toward the counter. When I shifted around it so I was in the small kitchen space with Alice, she peered over her shoulder with a look that screamed surprise.

"I can bring your drink into my—"

Before she said the final word, I cupped both sides of her face and brought her lips to mine. Hard. I kissed her like we hadn't kissed an hour ago on the floor of her bedroom. I kissed her without the push of a silly card game behind it. I kissed her not because I wanted to, but because I *needed* to.

If I walked away from her, toward those messages—as much as I knew I needed to—I would regret it. I couldn't walk away from a soul that was so forgiving and kind, but also so vibrant and fierce. I'd never been in a space with someone—under these circumstances either—who made me feel at ease the way I did with Alice...even when she was being passive aggressive as fuck. We'd only known each other for three hours, but during those three hours, I'd felt a small part of me change.

I couldn't walk away from that change.

Especially when it had come about so naturally.

Instead, I'd walk with this feeling...absorb it.

I took her in, tasting a hint of sugar on her tongue and smelling nutmeg flow off her clothes as she wrapped her hands around my neck. I pulled at the elastic of her skirt's waistband until her waist pressed against mine, the counter biting into the small of her back. Movements flowed without an ounce of effort—her bottom lip as I yanked at it gently between my teeth, the press of her hips against mine, my hands as I lifted her up onto the counter. Giggling, she carefully plucked the tablet off its dock and placed it on a shelf within arm's reach before facing me as I stood between her legs.

In only my boxer briefs and socks.

Boxer briefs that definitely looked a little tighter than before.

"Don't you...don't you want to message Kati?" she whispered, running soft fingers up and down my sides. I paused when she mentioned her name, my movements stiffening for only a second before I loosened up again.

"I'll get to that after," I said softly, lifting her chin up so her eyes fell into mine. They were as rich and dark as freshly brewed coffee. "First, I want this. I like *this*."

"I like this too...*Liam*." The way she said my name—even with that innocently flirtatious edge—made me grow harder as I stepped closer to her. Her legs wrapped around the back of mine, my rock-hard cock brushing the side of her thigh as I leaned closer. Her eyes darted down, and with an eyebrow raised, she said, "I can tell you like this."

I pulled her chin up a little more until my lips were only a breath away from hers. My free hand wandered up her leg, fingers whispering below her thin skirt until I finally felt the edge of her panties: barely there lace. I didn't want to move too quickly—even though after knowing each other for only a few hours, this was warped speed—but I had to touch her. Taste her. She was too close not to consume. My eyes stayed locked on hers as I held her chin in place and said, "I can tell you do too."

I slipped a finger beneath the lace but only brushed over her sex, teasing her a little bit.

Hell, teasing *myself* a little bit.

I needed to feel how wet she was for me.

And when she let out a breathy gasp when I ran a finger over her clit, I knew that was it.

That was all I could take.

I pulled my finger from her panties—another gasp echoing through the café—and grabbed at each side of her skirt, pulling the elastic band down until her skirt hung at her ankles. She kicked off the skirt with a giggle, and I took a step back to absorb this picture of her sitting on the counter in nothing but red lace panties.

Red.

Lace.

Panties.

That were, quite obviously, already drenched.

And I could see right through them as I eyed her delectable pussy.

I wanted to lock this picture in the front of my mind to relive whenever anxiety flooded my body after too many meetings, or exhausting emails, or dates that didn't mean anything.

Right now, *this* meant something.

She meant something.

And I couldn't describe the feeling humming in my chest, but it was something I hadn't felt when planning to meet Kati or Stef or any of the girls I'd recently gone on dates with.

And even though I'd just become a faded memory to her, all I wanted was to keep feeling this buzzing behind my ribs.

Because it was electric.

And it was a feeling I hadn't felt in a long, long time.

Chapter Nine

Alice

M Y BARE ASS WAS on the counter, and I was wet as fuck.

I was surprised I hadn't slipped right off, the two of us crashing onto the espresso-stained hardwood floor. Instead, I sat there, watching Liam pull my skirt off of my ankles and toss it, his eyes never leaving mine as they stared intently through those dark-rimmed frames.

Fuck, I was in trouble.

I never should have let this guy into my apartment.

Because now, I was afraid I'd never want him to leave.

And he wasn't going to stay. Not in Holly Hill, not in any one town for long, and definitely not with me.

But what I *was* going to do was enjoy the fuck out of this—out of *him*.

Because how he looked planting light kisses along my inner thighs as his hands wrapped around to cup my ass was delicious.

"I want to taste you, Alice," he whispered, his five o'clock shadow causing goosebumps to flower my skin. His kisses paused as he got to my underwear, and he looked back up at me, his light eyes dark with need. "Plus...we're matching. Red. I *need* to taste what's underneath."

"Then taste me, Lucas." I giggled—proud I still had some L names in me—but that giggle transformed into a gasp when heat brushed over the red lace barely leaving anything to the imagination. Down on his knees in front of me, he grabbed my ass and pulled me closer so his face was directly between my thighs. My clit pulsed as he gently licked it, the fabric of my underwear creating a devilish barrier between us.

I was great with eye contact when it came to everyday life, but when it came to this—anything intimate where I didn't have the reins—my eyes slammed shut. I escaped from reality and dove into a totally different world where my body could feel and writhe and roll. Eye contact during moments like this terrified me for reasons I couldn't pinpoint. Maybe it was a mix of my insecurities and doubts coming to the surface while I still felt empowered and wild. Maybe if I looked the person in the eye as they made me feel completely at ease, I'd feel undeserving of it all.

Maybe I felt guilty for feeling good when I knew it could all change in an instant.

But this instant felt different. I wanted to truly feel the emotions and vibrations buzzing inside of me without thoughts of guilt or doubt. Though my eyes stayed shut, I ran my fingers through Liam's bright auburn hair as he hummed against my clit. I wanted to rip that lace off and chuck it into the fire growling behind us. The separation was such beautiful torture.

He pulled the edge of my panties away with his teeth just for them to snap back to where they'd been seconds before.

I needed to take control.

I needed him to make me come right here on the counter of my fucking coffee shop.

A counter I'd forever see in a different light once tonight was over.

"Oh my god, you cannot do that again without pulling them off, Liam."

This time, I did open my eyes when I said the words. I met his gaze, my panties still between his teeth as he mumbled, "You said my name again."

"I sure as hell did," I whimpered, running a finger from the roots of his hair down to his chin. It was my turn to play this game. "And since I *did* say your name, I need you to take my panties off with your teeth and fuck me with your tongue. You got that, *Liam?*"

It was as if I was looking right into the eyes of a puppy—a puppy on the verge of becoming a wolf.

And boy did that wolf come to life.

Immediately, Liam yanked the lace down my legs, forcing me to adjust my spot on the counter so they could slide fully off. He flung them toward my skirt and leaned forward, his hands cupping my ass again, nails digging into the bare flesh.

I leaned back onto my elbows, widening my legs so he could see every inch of my damp pussy that was screaming for him. He ran a finger from the hem of my oversized top down to my belly button and then to my clit, rolling his fingertip over it before continuing the motion down to my entrance. He hovered just outside of it and moved his face closer, blowing a breath of cool air over my sex until my head fell back in beautiful agony.

"I think...I think you're truly trying to murder me, *Levi*," I whispered, flipping my head back up so blonde strands fell in front of my eyes. "I think this is how I go."

"Well, you can't go without coming for me," Liam said, his voice hushed at almost a growl. "But I won't taste you or touch you any more until you say my name."

"Your name?" I asked, my breathing heavy. "Your *real* name?"

Liam laughed. "You're a fucking tease, you know that?"

"I think *you're* the one doing the teasing, Luke."

He let out another whisper of breath over my sex, and I shuddered, my knuckles whitening against the counter. "Say it."

"Say *your* name?" I asked, angry at myself for playing this game but also loving every second of it.

Another gust of cool air fell over my clit, and the pulse became wicked as I watched his finger grow closer to my entrance. "Say my fucking name, Alice."

"Liam!" I shouted desperately, my voice echoing through the room as the lights flickered above us, wind howling against the storefront windows.

Liam chuckled, quickly removing his glasses with a sly grin. "There's my good girl. Now, open those legs wider for me. I need you to come all over this damn counter."

For a millisecond, I thought about how frustrating it would be sanitizing the counter the next day.

But before I could overthink, my back arched, and I let out a squeal as sensation filled my body. Liam plunged two fingers inside of me, cool air blowing over my clit until I felt the tip of his tongue circle my bundle of nerves. Both of his hands were now wrapped around my thighs, opening them as wide as they could go as he licked and fingered my pussy.

I'd never had an orgasm in my coffee shop, let alone on the counter right next to the drip coffee machine and a cup of cold espresso leftover from the martinis.

How unsanitary.

But how incredibly *hot*.

And we needed some heat during this snowstorm.

How he curled his fingers so they twisted inside of me with such ease while sucking on my clit simultaneously was a rhythm I couldn't explain. My body hummed, my core tightening with each stroke of his tongue and each movement of his fingers. My hands raked through his hair as I began gently thrusting forward against his face, a motion I could tell he enjoyed because I could feel his smile grow against my pussy.

"Fuck my face, Alice," Liam said. The break he took to talk was one second too long. My body was screaming for him to keep going. "I want to see those big eyes roll to the back of your head when you soak me."

"Jesus Christ," I said, pushing the back of his head back toward my pussy.

"It's Liam," he said with a smirk.

The second I grinned and turned away from his gaze, sinking into the vibration his tongue was causing, I felt a hand caress the side of my cheek. Looking up at me with eyes I could fall into, he said, "Watch me, Alice. I want to see those eyes."

"I'm only good at eye contact...when I'm working," I panted, rolling my hips as he twisted his wrist to hit the spot that made me immediately melt into the counter.

There was maybe a minute left before I couldn't hold myself together anymore.

I, honestly, didn't want to hold myself together anymore.

"Just pretend I'm one of your customers, Alice." Liam's voice came out as a grumble, vibrating between my legs. "I mean...I *was* one of your customers. So, this shouldn't be too hard to do."

"I see something that *is* noticeably hard that *I* want to do," I said, eyeing between his legs to see quite the bulge in his boxer briefs.

Nails bit into the sides of my thighs as he quickly flicked my clit with his tongue, the motions of his fingers moving faster inside of me.

Though I wanted to look away—simply because I'd conditioned myself to avoid this kind of eye contact—I did everything I could not to. I watched as Liam's breathing grew tense alongside mine. I watched as he fingered me harder and sucked on my clit to add more pressure. I watched until it felt like my entire body had caught fire, and I couldn't hold back anymore.

"Holy shit, holy shit. Liam, I'm coming," I shouted, biting my bottom lip and shutting my eyes tight as my head fell back. I pressed his face closer to my pussy, and with one more swipe of his tongue, I fell apart on that counter.

Hot energy swarmed my trembling body as my toes curled, and I clutched Liam's hair with such force I was surprised he didn't flinch.

The pulsing sensation in my core kept growing and building and flowing through me with such intensity.

I never wanted it to end.

I wanted to feel like I was floating forever.

I released my grip, and Liam leaned away from me, licking his lips and smiling up at me with a hint of pride in his eyes. He looked over his shoulder and then underneath the counter I was sitting on until he found the small mini fridge I kept back here. "There's got to be water in here. I think you are a bit dehydrated now, huh?"

"Shut your face," I said, rolling my eyes with a giggle.

He wasn't wrong.

I hadn't come like that in...well, *years*.

"I have to restock the fridge, but tap water is fine." I looked around the counter for a glass I could grab for him without my lazy ass having to move. But as I scanned the space, my gaze fell upon the small demitasse cup I'd put the leftover espresso into when making the martinis.

It was as if the glorious russet liquid was smiling up at me.

Something about it must have inspired me because, suddenly, I felt feral.

"Get on your back," I demanded with a playful edge clinging to each word.

Liam, still down on his knees, looked up at me with furrowed brows as he put his glasses back on. "Excuse me?"

"Get on your back."

"Right...here?"

I gestured toward the rug in front of the fireplace. "Over there is fine."

"Um...okay," he said, getting to his feet, slowly wandering toward the fireplace.

"You said you were thirsty, yes?" I asked hopping off the counter with the espresso cup in hand.

Liam knelt down on the rug, his cock at full mast against his boxer briefs. "I said *you're* probably thirsty."

Placing the cup on the counter to slip my lace underwear back on, I grabbed it again and slowly made my way to the fireplace. "That's correct. I am... I'm parched, but I'm also quite hungry."

His eyes darted from the demitasse cup in my hand, to my eyes, then back to the cup again. "Okay...can I help you with this problem?"

Giggling, I swiped the tiny blonde braid dangling in front of my face behind my ear and took the tiniest sip of the cold espresso. "Yes. I think you can."

CHAPTER TEN

Liam

S HE WAS LOOKING DOWN at me as if she was going to eat me in one bite.

But why was she holding a cup of our leftover espresso?

And why did her smile look so damn wicked?

"How can I help you, Alice?" I asked softly, her eyes darkening as she came down to kneel in front of me. The fire crackled behind us, the wind still trying to break through the storefront door and windows.

Alice gently circled the espresso in the cup. "Get on your back."

I did as I was told.

"Good," she whispered, finally setting the cup down on a chair beside her. She quickly pushed my legs apart so she was staring directly at my brief-covered cock, and she slid her hands up my calves and thighs until she was right at the edge of my boxer briefs. Her soft lips pressed against the skin right near the elastic, and goosebumps covered every inch of me. With each kiss, I felt myself growing harder as my heart did a wild dance in my chest.

She carefully lowered my boxer briefs until the red fabric pooled at my ankles before I kicked it off. The grin on her face was almost demonic—especially on a face so sweet and pure.

If I'd learned anything tonight, it was that the sweet façade many people wore only hid darker, deeper thoughts and memories they didn't want to face.

Or at least face alone.

She placed two hands over my chest—not without giggling at my damn nipple rings—before sliding them down over my core and to my hips. Her eyes had now shifted to my cock between her arms, almost touching her chest. "Well...I knew you were a big boy, but I didn't expect *this*."

"I'm not sure how to take that," I laughed, lifting my head off the floor so I could see her better. And fuck, did she look beautiful with the fireplace light bouncing off her face and bare legs. "But thank you."

"You're *very* welcome," Alice sang, reaching for the espresso demitasse. "I think you'll also thank me after my playtime with you is over."

"Over? I don't want it to be—"

"Playtime isn't over. It's happening right *now*," Alice explained, wagging her free hand at my chest until my head was back flat on the ground. "Now don't move. You'll have to use my shower after this...but I think you'll be okay with that."

"What are you about to do?" I asked, already liking the position she was in above my center.

"Are you okay with getting a little messy tonight, Mr. Put-Together?" Alice asked this in the softest, yet sultriest voice I'd ever fucking heard.

Did I like making a mess? No.

Did I often become an angry barbarian when my clothes were wrinkled or stained? Yes.

But right now, I was lying on a woven rug wearing only my socks with a woman I'd just met but felt like I'd known for years.

I had no reason to get uptight or worried...and from the looks of it, I *definitely* was more than comfortable around her.

"I'll get a little messy with you, Alice," I whispered, cupping her thighs and pressing my fingers into the soft flesh. "I just want to know why you're holding that—"

And before I could get the last word out, a cold sensation hit me. Cold and wet and dripping. Alice was slowly pouring the espresso from the cup onto my belly and trailing it down until it was dripping over my cock. She'd placed her free hand at the base, pressure flowing through her fingers as they wrapped around me, espresso dripping over her hand.

For a moment, I lay there in shock.

Had this woman *really* just poured cold espresso over my body?

Over my fucking dick, nonetheless?

It brought me back to how furious I felt when the date I'd had the month before accidentally knocked her red wine all over my suit. It brought me back to when I'd had to push a date's car out of mud after an outdoor concert, and I'd been livid about the mud stains on my new jeans.

Yes, they'd just been jeans...but they'd been *new*.

But this. This felt different. This time—unlike our experience on the counter—her eyes were on mine every second she poured the liquid over me. Her grin was so teasing, a mix of innocence and defiance crowding her face. From my spot on the floor—somehow, I kept ending up down here—all I could see was her energy radiating around us.

Her spunk.

Her excitement.

Her confidence.

I could feel all of that and more the second she took control of this espresso scenario.

I wanted to bathe in the energy she was releasing.

Instead, I was bathing in espresso.

"Jesus Christ," I whispered, watching as the final drop slid down from head to shaft to base.

"It's *Alice*," she said back in a hushed tone, a clever eyebrow raised. As she set the cup aside, her other hand began moving up and down my length in a twisting motion.

I'd expected the espresso to make everything stickier—and I was *not* a fan of being sticky. From how this felt—and it felt damn good—it only made my cock that much slicker against her palms.

"Holy shit...I didn't expect this to feel as good as it does," I said, balancing on my forearms so I could watch this espresso art continue.

Giggling one of those wicked giggles, she lowered her face to just above my espresso-covered cock. She smiled down at it before looking me directly in the eyes and licking the very tip, savoring the taste.

I'd always thought espresso was a little bitter.

And cold espresso couldn't taste all that great—unless in an iced dirty chai or espresso martini.

Maybe this was just the best way to consume it.

"If you think *this* feels good…I bet I can make you feel even better," she said, licking the tip again. This time, she didn't stop at the tip. She continued licking all the way down to the base, not stopping until she was softly licking my balls, her lips wrapping around them like they were the sweetest candy. After giving them a few licks, her tongue continued its path back up my shaft and to the head of my cock that was now covered in espresso and pre-cum.

I was already about to fucking lose it.

"Yes…" I whimpered as she circled the tip of me with that talented tongue of hers. "Make me feel better, Alice."

Looking up at me with a mischievous gaze, she said, "I'm good at taking orders."

I tried to respond, but my breath hitched the second I felt her devour my cock, both hands twisting as she sucked up and down. The movements of her tongue against my shaft forced a low moan to escape as I went back to lying flat on the floor, removing my glasses and setting them by the fireplace. I reached for the back of her head as she moved at a faster speed, and I pressed her farther down onto me, my body jolting against her pretty little face.

One thing that impressed me—just as much as her excellent tongue skills—was her ability to maintain eye contact.

She'd avoided my eyes at all costs when I'd gone down on her.

But now that she was in control, it was as if she'd switched into a totally different version of herself—one that didn't come out to play very often.

I was so damn glad I'd helped prepare this version of her for playtime.

"Just like that…yes." I panted, feeling my core tighten with each movement. "Good girl, Alice. You're being such a good, good girl. I'm so fucking close."

"You're close, huh?" she asked, releasing her lips from my cock for a second.

"Yes, yes…I am. Don't stop. Don't fucking stop."

Alice circled her tongue at the head of my cock before saying, "Well, then come for me, Liam."

And that was it.

Before she had time to wrap her lips back around my cock, I covered her hand with mine at the base, and came. I came harder than I thought was even possible. We both stroked up and down, my hand over hers as I pulsed within our grasp. Beads of cum collided with her sweater, her shoulder, her chin, and cheeks and she just knelt there, with a smile, taking me in as I fell apart in front of her.

Our hands released, and she sat back, giggling to herself as she wiped some cum from her neck. "Well…I deserved that."

I lay flat on the floor, my chest still lifting and falling at warped speed. "Deserved what?"

"To get just as messy as you are," she stated, licking her cum-covered finger. "It wouldn't have been fair for you to get all dirty without me joining in a little bit."

"And you liked joining in? Getting a little messy?" I asked, lifting back onto my forearms so I could look her dead in those saucer-shaped eyes I couldn't stop falling into.

She wiped a little cum off her sweater dangling off one shoulder, followed by some from her cheek. "Why play it safe? This, right here, is peak playtime. Espresso and all."

"And the cold espresso *actually* tasted good?" I asked, finally getting an answer to the question I'd wondered about.

Alice shrugged. "It was a good garnish—a little bitter, but good. It was the main dessert that *really* hit the taste buds."

And then she winked.

I swore I could have melted.

Or maybe it was the fire at my back making me feel warm all over again.

"Well..." I said, trying to kick myself out of my head as I came to a seated position. "We're *both* a bit dirty here...so, we probably should—"

"Shower."

I watched Alice get to her feet and wiggle her little lace-covered ass as she stood in place. Her energy was electric...all the damn time.

"Yeah." I got to my feet and, standing naked in front of the fireplace—some dried espresso still coating my skin—I said, "A shower is a great idea."

CHAPTER ELEVEN

Alice

AFTER I SHOWED LIAM where I kept the extra towels and he closed the bathroom door, I collapsed onto my bed with arms wide open. Lying on my quilt with only my off-the-shoulder top and lace underwear on, I felt so free. So completely at ease.

I hadn't felt like I was floating in so long.

I probably hadn't felt this way since my last boyfriend...who'd moved across the country two years ago. He'd wanted me to come with him—to explore the Rocky Mountains and really see how clear night skies could be, but I couldn't leave. There was no way I'd up and leave the business my parents put so much time into perfecting.

I couldn't do that to them.

A brush of soft fur tickled my foot as Archibald jumped up onto the bed, releasing a pitchy meow that sounded more like nails on a chalkboard than a demand for me to pet him. Alas, I scratched his neck—the way I did every night—until the shower turned off and the door handle twisted.

It had taken everything in me not to jump into that shower with him.

We probably needed some space—if space was possible when you were snowed into a small studio like we were. I didn't want to hover or seem needy, even though I wanted to feel his breath on my skin and dive into his cinnamon scent again. But I knew, in a few hours, the snow would slow, and he would leave Holly Hill.

Maybe he'd stop in when passing through next time. Hell, maybe this would all happen again next year when swinging by on his way to his family's holiday party.

But next year, he'd be well on his way to marriage at the rate he was going.

So, was there any use dreaming?

"Good shower pressure, and this towel feels brand new," Liam said as he stepped out in the red boxer briefs still begging to be stared at. He was drying his dark, rust-colored hair with a teal towel when he noticed who was lying at my side. "Is that an Archibald?"

Archibald let out a hiss and rolled to his other side, curling into my armpit. "It is an Archibald."

"He looks angry. Like...his face is all squished into one spot. That *has* to anger him."

My jaw dropped. "Lark, do *not* insult the world's finest Persian cat. He is royalty."

Liam rolled his eyes and finished drying his hair, wrapping the towel around his shoulders like a neck pillow. "You're next. I'll keep the king company."

"Good. He still doesn't trust you, though. Be on your best behavior," I said, standing up and walking to the bathroom, nudging his arm as I passed.

The shower was a needed reset, the hot water rinsing away any unnecessary emotions clinging to my thoughts. But when I turned the water off and slipped into my favorite silk pajamas—the ones I only wore on rare *special* occasions—I opened the door to find Liam sitting at my desk, the laptop flipped open. The screen was bright, and it was quite obvious he was scrolling an inbox—*not* an email. From the coffee cup logo at the corner, I could tell it was the My Cup o' Joe dating app he'd mentioned earlier that evening.

The one Kati was on.

He was being a good person by updating her on the situation.

But why was my stomach twisting into knots?

"I see the laptop is working," I said, wishing I could take back my passive-aggressive tone.

Liam looked over his shoulder, Archibald staring at him from the corner of my bed. "Yeah. I thought I'd do a little catch-up while you showered. Are you feeling better?"

I felt much better when I was coming all over your face in the café.

"Yeah," I mumbled, walking over to my bed and slouching down into the fluffy comforter, Archibald finally trekking away from his security guard spot. "I'm fine."

This was when Liam twisted toward me in the swivel chair, leaning forward over his knees. "You're *fine?*"

I nodded and pulled the comforter to right below my chin, blonde hair scattering over my pillow.

"Well, I don't believe *that* for one second," Liam said with a laugh.

"Why not? Feeling fine is great."

"You don't seem like a person to describe yourself as feeling *fine*," Liam said, scooting the swivel chair a little closer to the bed. "Maybe *superb* and *terrific*, but not *fine*."

"Do I really seem like a *superb* girl?"

"You do."

Well, that was something I'd never been called.

I didn't hate it.

"I honestly hate when people say they're *fine*," I admitted, twisting to the side and pulling the comforter tighter below my chin. "There's always some negative connotation behind it."

"So, you admit it?"

"Admit what?" I asked.

"That you're not actually fine," Liam muttered, lifting an eyebrow in triumph.

"Ughhhh, you're the worst!" I flipped over to the other side. "Go sleep in Archibald's bed by the bathroom door. It's the little cardboard box with the pillow."

Liam snickered, and the edge of my bed shifted as he climbed onto it. "Why are you *fine*'ing me?"

I stayed silent.

Well, sort of. I let out a fake snore.

I felt Liam's hand wrap around my ankle—impressed he was able to find it with my body all scrunched up under the comforter. "Alyssa..."

"I can't handle the name game when it's the other way around." I immediately sat up, crossing my legs beneath me with the comforter still covering my bottom half. "Did you message Kati?"

He nodded. "I did."

"Is she mad you missed the date?"

He shook his head. "She understood. We're getting coffee at Java Jude's in Merlin tomorrow morning once the snow clears."

I slowly nodded, my head doing an awkward wave. "Neat."

"Are you...jealous?" Liam asked. "Are you jealous of Kati and me? Because you shouldn't be. We just—"

"You're right. *We* just met. It's so, *so* silly for me to be getting all fuzzy and warm thinking about a nonexistent reality where you don't magically disappear tomorrow. I've just had fun tonight, and I don't get to have this much fun often and—"

"Alice." Liam's hand gently cupped my chin, and I looked up to see his intent gaze washing over my flushed body. "I was going to say *we,* as in Kati and I, just started talking a couple weeks ago. It isn't serious...but it *is* something I'm going to explore. My brother is really excited about this date, and with everything coming up, it could be something that works."

"But are *you* excited?"

Liam paused, releasing his hand from my chin. "I mean, I know it's something that could be good long-term. I want to stay more grounded with someone who understands I will have to still travel from time to time for long spurts."

"You didn't answer my question, Lorenzo."

"Will this name thing ever end?"

I quickly shook my head. "Nope."

"Well, if you want *honesty,* this date with Kati feels a little forced, at this point. I think once I meet her, it won't feel this way. Then I'll feel some genuine excitement." He sighed, leaning onto his wrist. He pushed his chin in my direction with a smirk. "What about you? When was the last date you went on?"

I snorted out a laugh so loud I swear the lights flickered. "A date? Ha! You're such a jokester."

"Now *you* didn't answer my question."

"Because I'm trying to sleep." I slumped back onto the comforter cocoon, nodding toward the bathroom door. "Remember? The cat bed is yours."

"Are you *really* going to make me sleep in a cat bed?" he asked, looking at it over his shoulder. "It does look cozy, though. I mean, I'd never want you to feel uncomfortable either way. I'd be fine snuggling up by the fire out in the café."

"I put out the fire when you were in the shower," I said flatly. "I'm quick. Very sneaky."

"You truly are one of Santa's elves." His hand returned to my ankle once I'd stretched my legs back out under the covers. "But really. Why do you laugh when I ask you about dating? I'm sure you could get any guy in this town to swoon over you."

"Yeah, until they leave." The air stilled around us, even the snow seeming to grow still.

"You've hinted at this theme a few times," Liam said, giving my ankle a tiny squeeze that I ignored. "Why do you keep saying this?"

"Because no one just *stays* in Holly Hill," I whispered at a volume I swore only my pillow could hear. "The only people who stay are those tied down because of family or specific passions or love. My family is gone, so I am continuing their dream for them. Passions...coffee. Coffee and making my family proud—even in death. And when it comes to love...love continues to prove to me that it doesn't stick around."

"So, you feel stuck?"

The air in my lungs hitched. Hearing the truth come from someone else's mouth was a reality I hadn't faced yet. It was one I hadn't thought I'd have to face. "I do."

"Then...why can't you find a different way to continue your family's dream? Get creative with it in some way."

I scoffed, tightening my grip on the comforter and pulling it below my chin again. "Yeah, okay. I'll just sell the place and go travel the state—the world—drinking other people's coffee and buying other people's art to pile into some camper."

"I mean...that doesn't sound like a bad idea, Alice."

I twisted to face Liam, my brow furrowed. "If I'd answered their call that night, Liam, maybe I could have left and traveled and fallen in love, but I didn't. I didn't answer the call, and now they're gone. They built this place from the ground up, and now the most I can do is live out their dream for them since I stopped them from living it themselves. My love for them overpowers a love I've never had with anyone else, and if that's the only love I ever get to feel, so be it."

Silence hugged both of us, tense and unforgiving.

The snow howled against the windows, the single light by the small kitchen table flickering and rocking in place.

Maybe the moon, the stars, the earth did pull energy from us all.

Because nature could feel the energy building inside of me—an energy I wasn't familiar with. It wasn't anger. It wasn't sadness.

It felt more like shame.

"Alice..." Liam whispered, his voice almost disappearing into the wind's angry song. "This wasn't your fault. You can't keep putting that weight on your shoulders. You deserve...you deserve to live the life *you* want. Your parents would want that for you. They'd want you to feel that...and find love."

I pulled my ankle away from his grasp. "Yeah...well, then find me someone who isn't just passing through town on their way to something better."

When I eyed him from my cocoon of sheets, I could tell that one stung.

He sat there, still shirtless in his red boxer briefs with his auburn hair damp. He wasn't smiling. He wasn't grimacing. He was just...there.

Taking it all in.

Taking in a night of emotions he never expected to take in.

His bare feet found the hardwoods, and he made his way to the light in the kitchen, flicking it off. When the studio went dark, I closed my eyes too, pressing them together with such force I hoped the pressure would stop tears from forming. I rarely cried and didn't need this to be when the dam finally broke.

But when I heard the sound of cardboard adjusting over the floor and a soft whine come from Liam as he squished himself onto a circular pillow, I couldn't help but let out a tearful laugh.

Especially when Archibald was hissing from his spot beneath my sheets.

"Just...don't," I whimpered, masking a giggle wrapped in unwanted tears. I shifted closer to the wall as Archibald flew out from the sheets back into the depths under my bed. Obviously, he didn't want to venture to his cat bed being rented out against his will.

"It's...cozy," Liam said. "I'm fine."

"You're not," I said, flipping open the comforter. "Just get in. Stay...stay three feet away. Remember?"

"That'll be impossible if we're in the same full-size bed together."

I patted the mattress beside me, doing all I could to suck the tears back into my eyes. I would *not* go to bed with tears staining my pillowcase, especially if this giant of a man was about to steal the sheets from me all night.

A man who'd made me feel every emotion on the spectrum over the last three hours and still had the ability to pull a laugh out of me.

"*Emotionally*, stay three feet away," I said, my eyes linking to Liam's through the darkness. "Please...please just come to bed."

"I *am* in a bed."

I sighed, rolling my eyes. "Lie next to me, Liam."

CHAPTER TWELVE

Liam

Every time she said my name—my *actual* name—I swear I came apart.

So, when she beckoned me over to her bed, I couldn't resist. I mean, anything was a better option than the world's tiniest cardboard box bed she'd made for Archibald. The effort and creativity were there, but the comfort absolutely was not.

As I scooted beneath the comforter and she shifted over to give me more space, I realized just how much I felt for her. This woman—this wild, spunky woman—was pushing away a future within her grasp. She had every opportunity to explore and travel and fall in love, but guilt was weighing her down.

I, on the other hand, wanted to feel weighed down to one location for more than a month at a time.

Hell, I'd take staying in one place for more than a couple weeks at a time at this point. The only time I ever felt completely set in one place was when the shows were shooting, and I was on location. That only happened three or four months out of each year, and even then, I was running around like a lunatic.

I was on the search for stability while she was searching for freedom.

We were magnets shooting in opposite directions.

But still, we found ourselves sharing the same bed in a studio inside her family's café. Though our magnetic pull was anything but, we still found ourselves being pulled by some force we couldn't explain.

Maybe it was the snow forcing us into one place.

Maybe it was our trauma dumps making us feel closer than we would with any other stranger.

But whatever it was, I liked it.

I just knew I shouldn't.

"You're a furnace," Alice whispered, lying on her side with only those big eyes of hers peeking over the covers.

I shrugged, turning onto my side to face her. "You're welcome."

"Who says I *want* to be warm? Maybe I'm a furnace too, and what I need is a fridge."

"Look outside, Alice," I muttered, nodding toward the windows surrounding us. "Being a furnace is a blessing."

"Hmmph." She curled into her comforter some more. "You're only in this bed because I can't fathom you sleeping in Archibald's."

"It wasn't *that* bad."

The tip of her toe brushed my shin, and she immediately shot her foot back. "Yeah...well...you're lucky."

"I am." Our eyes were lasers, and I felt her toes tickle my shin again. Laughing and nudging my leg closer to her, I said, "Are you hinting at something?"

"I mean..." Alice mumbled, rolling her eyes. "I guess we can cuddle. Just to keep each other warm since you're *such* a furnace."

"I take it you're the fridge?"

Alice nodded. "Yeah...I run *very* cold. All the time. It's not great to always be cold in a place that's already always cold."

I shifted closer to her until her leg wrapped around my back, and she pulled herself flush against me. My arm wrapped around her waist and I brought her in closer until her head was against my chest. I felt her nudging the side of her face against me, the upturn of her lips against my skin.

"Larson?"

"Yes?"

"If I didn't have to stay put...like, if I could travel...would you go on a date with me like the one you're having with Kati tomorrow?"

I rolled my eyes in the darkness, hoping she couldn't see. "You truly can step away if you want...and stop comparing yourself to Kati. I already know you better than I know her. I just...I need to follow through with the date and meet her. I'm not good at bailing."

"You didn't answer my question." She looked up at me through the darkness as a sliver of light cascaded across her face. "Would you go on a date with me?"

"Alice, I see tonight as being our first date. Even if...even *when* I do leave, I still see tonight as being our first date. So, the answer is yes."

Her eyes practically glowed through the black. "Really?"

"Yes."

The corners of her lips pinched. "What about if the card game was our first date, the café escapades were our second date, and this right here is our third?"

"I mean, sure. But why do they need to be numbered?"

She giggled, her arm finding my waist as she pushed herself hard against me. "Because by the third date, my clothes would definitely be off. And I don't want to keep them—or yours—on right now...even though you're annoying me."

And...great.

I was already halfway hard.

"Well, if I'm annoying you...maybe we—"

Her lips hit mine, her fingertips clawing at my lower back as our tongues collided. My hands wandered down to her ass, and I cupped it hard, pressing myself against her as I felt her hips roll. She wasn't just slowly rolling against me. She was doing it with purpose, with passion. It was as if she didn't want to miss any time or let one more moment go to waste, because she knew, in the morning, time would keep on moving, and so would our lives.

I didn't want to waste another second either.

So, I would show her how badly I didn't want to leave in the morning.

I would show her how it felt to spend time with someone you adored—whether stuck in one place or traveling nonstop. When you adored someone, it didn't matter where you were.

It mattered who you were with—whether physically or in your heart.

And right now, Alice mattered.

"You're..." she started, one hand walking away from my waist and around to my thigh. "You're only annoying me a little bit."

"Only a *little* bit, huh?" Her nails raked up my thighs until arriving at the red boxer briefs holding my insanely hard cock in place. How was it even possible to get this hard *that* fast?

We'd only been kissing for, maybe, two minutes.

"Mm-hmm..." she hummed, cupping my bulge and gently grasping it as I pulsed in her hand. "You may be annoying me a little, but I know something that isn't little or annoying...and I want it."

She pulled the elastic of my boxer briefs down, and for the second time tonight, I kicked them off, losing them somewhere in the tangle of sheets. Her hand stroked up and down slowly, as if savoring every movement while also thoroughly teasing me. Her thumb softly rubbed the head of my cock as she planted kisses on my cheekbones and neck, her free hand crawling up into my hair.

"You want it?" I whispered.

She nodded against me, hair falling over her face as she continued to kiss and suck at my neck and earlobe. "I do. I want it."

"Then take it. Take me, Alice. Tonight, I'm yours."

Alice flung her body on top of me, the covers falling down so nothing and no one was hidden anymore. She reached beneath the edge of her pajama top and pulled it up and over her head, revealing a bare chest with perky, pink nipples staring directly at me. No red lace bra. No little strapless thing. Just beautiful tits that I couldn't wait to touch and taste.

"My god..." I whispered, pulling her chest toward my face so I could take a nipple into my mouth, flicking it with my tongue as her head fell back.

"Keep doing that with your tongue...holy shit," she demanded, rolling her hips against me with legs straddled. "And you can play a little rough with me. I like to be bitten."

Of course, I obeyed.

I took her nipple between my teeth, pulling it until her eyes rolled back, and she bit her lip, her hips never slowing their motion. Those pajama shorts and that little lace fabric between us was going to have to go soon, because I was already about to lose my shit just watching her lose hers.

"Yup. Yes...that feels *so* fucking good," Alice moaned. "Your tongue. Your teeth. Your glasses. Your fucking nipple piercings. Stop being so nerdy and so...so hot."

Well, damn.

She was dry humping the fuck out of me while spewing compliments.

I needed to be inside of her.

I finagled my fingers into her golden mess of hair and brought her face closer to mine, adding pressure to my grip as I whispered, "Now, take off those shorts and those panties before I rip them all straight off that tight little body of yours."

She giggled as I released her hair. "Yes, sir."

She got up onto her feet so she was standing above me, her body towering over me like the most beautiful skyscraper. Her thumbs wiggled into the hem of her shorts and panties, and she slid them both down her thighs until she had to readjust her stance to take them off her ankles.

And my God. This view.

This fucking view was decadent.

Her delicate landing strip.

Her lips begging to be tasted.

I saw her pussy an hour or so before, but nothing compared to this view.

"Sit on my face. Now," I demanded, my mouth watering as I flung my glasses onto the floor by the bed. "Before you feel me inside of you, I need to taste you again."

Another round of those giggles made her tits bounce as she stepped forward the slightest bit. "I mean...if you insist."

"I absolutely insist."

As she stood above my face, I grabbed her thighs and pulled her down onto me. I didn't hesitate a single second, immediately grasping her thighs tighter and licking up her folds to find her clit. I wrapped my lips around that sensitive bundle of nerves and began to suck, lapping my tongue around it every few seconds so I could feel her twitch against my face.

Every twitch sent a spark of pleasure straight to my cock.

Fuck, I wanted this woman.

Needed her.

"Holy shit, I'm going to come already," Alice whimpered, rolling her hips against my lips as I continued to suck and tease.

I looked up at her, only for her to look away with an adorable grin, and said, "It's been, like, one minute."

"Well, I'm fucking sensitive, okay?" She huffed out a laugh as she pushed herself closer to my face. "Keep doing that thing with your tongue. Don't fucking stop, Liam."

And I could never disobey *that* command.

I went back to the rhythm I'd been doing seconds before—sucking and circling, sucking and circling. She rode my face harder, determination radiating off her as she continued to play with her nipples with one hand, the other hand raking through her hair. Her hips began to quicken just for them to completely stop, but that didn't mean I was stopping.

I knew from the tension in her legs and that wild look in her eyes that she was about come all over my face for the second time tonight.

And, my God, I couldn't wait to taste it.

"Oh my god, oh my god, Liam...holy shit!" Alice shouted, leaning forward so she was clutching her bedframe as she trembled and dripped over my lips. I smiled against her as she continued to shake and pant and moan until she loosened her grip on the bedframe and collapsed into a puddle beside me, one leg still over my center.

"Oh, do you think we're done?" I whispered. "That's cute."

"I don't think...I have anything left in me," she said softly, out of breath. But as the last few words were said, she met my eyes for the first time since I'd pulled her down onto my face. Her exhausted features transformed into savage ones as she said, "But what I do want in me, is you."

Chapter Thirteen

Alice

I WAS EXHAUSTED FROM my second orgasm of the night—something I knew I shouldn't complain about—but I wasn't ready for this to be over. I didn't want it to end. I wanted to keep twisting in the sheets with Liam and keep feeling his touch and smelling his cinnamon scent.

There was something about this night—this night filled with heavy snowflakes, and a stirring fire, and cold espresso—making me want to open myself up even more than I already had. I was an extrovert who often talked too much but also kept private thoughts to myself. I didn't like the idea of burdening other people with the stressors bouncing around in my head, especially when most of them were rooted to my parents and the café.

I preferred to control my worries and thoughts and put them in a box to open when necessary—or when forced to face them.

But tonight didn't feel forced.

Tonight felt comfortable.

And for the first time in a long time, I wanted to keep that box open.

Liam sat up, his thumb brushing my chin as I lay on my back. "I absolutely did not bring any condoms."

"You don't have a condom pocket in that fancy jacket of yours?"

"Do most people have fancy condom pockets?"

"Maybe you should make it a thing," I giggled, running my hand from my neck to my chest to my belly before finding my clit, circling my fingers over it gently—teasingly. His eyes watched my every movement, completely absorbing me as he sat there hard as a rock. "Go check the café bathroom in the third drawer under the sugar cookie-scented lotion."

His eyes practically bulged out of his head. "Excuse me?"

"You're excused."

"There really may be a condom in your café bathroom?"

I shrugged, my fingers still circling. Fuck, I was teasing myself too much. "I found a bunch at a table when I was cleaning up about a month ago. I panicked and quickly put them in there so I could keep cleaning."

Liam was silent for a second, his eyes darting from me to my hand. Biting his lip, he said, "That's wild. I'll go look."

He stood up and walked butt naked through the door leading into the café. Never had I imagined a man this gorgeous—and this naked—to walk around my coffee shop at one in the morning on a search for condoms.

But, alas, here we were.

He returned and closed the door behind him, already ripping open the package with his teeth and sliding it over his hard length. I applied more pressure to myself as I watched him do this all while walking—almost gliding—toward the bed with such determination. His face was so serious but not without a hint of playfulness curling at the corners of his lips.

He crawled onto the bed, hovering above me with one hand by the side of my head and the other around himself. "I didn't expect this to be what happened when you fell into my arms in the bathroom."

I snorted out a laugh, sliding my hand up my body to my lips as he pressed himself against my entrance. Oh my God, did I want to feel him slide inside of me. I was already on the verge of losing it *again* within the span of a minute. "I never expected I'd fall into the arms of someone so dapper while taking the garbage out."

He grinned, the tip of his cock so close to slipping inside. The tease was both delicious and torturous.

"I need to feel you, Alice," Liam hummed, planting kisses on my neck leading up to my ear. His lips were velvet, hot against my skin. "I need to feel *all* of you."

"Then feel me, Liam," I said softly. "I need you to feel me *now*."

And then he pushed himself inside of me. He thrusted with an energy I couldn't pinpoint. Was it passion? Was it determination? Was it maybe something else?

No.

We'd known each other for maybe five hours.

He was fucking me because it felt fucking good.

No emotions attached.

Deeper and deeper, I felt him push inside of me. "Jesus Christ, Liam."

"You keep...calling me that tonight," he huffed, stopping deep and watching my head fall back with a moan. A cry of pleasure fell over my lips, and I bit the bottom one as I faced him.

His eyes.

They were bright lights burning right through me—seeing me.

All of me.

I didn't know what he was thinking or what he was *really* looking at when his eyes met mine. Into *just* my eyes? My thoughts? My emotions?

I looked to the side, avoiding the reality behind his emerald stare. "Well...you must be my religion. I'd absolutely pray to you."

He pushed his hips flush against mine, and I felt him deeper than he'd been even seconds before. I clawed at his strong back muscles, leaning forward to dig my teeth playfully into his deltoid. Wincing with a chuckle, he began moving again as our bodies fell into a beautifully unforced rhythm. I kissed his shoulder and neck as he pushed deep inside, curling his hips upward until I felt him hit right where I knew I'd lose all control.

Control.

It was such a bittersweet thing.

It was something I'd had to cling to over the last few years but also learn to let go of.

Because some things you just couldn't have control over.

"Alice." His voice was low, hushed even. I felt his finger at my chin, his hip motions slowing and circular as he lifted my gaze to meet his. "Look at me."

At first, I simply smiled, diverting my gaze toward one of the many windows covered in white. But I knew I couldn't fool him much longer. "You feel so—"

"Alice..."

I slowly faced Liam, my dark eyes meeting his light ones as our chests quickly lifted and fell in sync. "Liam."

"I want you to look at me when you come. I want to see you let go."

I began turning my head to the side, the pressure inside of me stirring in my core with every circle of his hips. "You're so damn—"

His hand gently directed my gaze back to his, and this time, I let myself truly look back at him. "It's okay to let go. Let go of that control, and let me take the reins."

Our breathing was heavy.

His movements deep and delicious.

Our frantic hearts meeting each other, chest to chest.

And for the first time in a long time, I poured myself into his gaze.

I poured myself into *him*.

I didn't look away when his movements sped up, my nerves electric. He continued to thrust and push and curl his body so, with every movement, I felt the most intense ping of pleasure all while his eyes were locked to mine. It was a buzzing sensation taking over my limbs and my mind and my heart. When I couldn't hold it in any longer, when I knew I was about to lose all control, I felt his body jolt against mine with release, forcing my own to completely come undone.

His warm, giant body hovered over me as his lips found mine, and one hand cupped the side of my face. "You're beautiful, Alice. You and your beautiful soul."

"Isn't that a song lyric from the early 2000s?"

Liam brushed his hand along the side of the bed and found his glasses, sliding them onto his stunned face. Laughing and shaking his head, he said, "Did you really just have to bring that up when we were having a *moment*?"

Giggling, I placed a hand on either side of his face. "Did you really put your glasses back on when you're about to fall asleep?"

I felt him slide out of me—but not without the two of us sighing in unison—and we both lay next to each other as he took the glasses back off his nose. "Touché. Let's get some sleep."

CHAPTER FOURTEEN

Liam

I DIDN'T KNOW IT was possible for slowing snowfall to wake me up.

Maybe it was the calming of the wind.

Maybe the wall of white was finally crumbling.

Maybe it was the silence that forced my eyes open.

Alice was curled into my side, her arm over my center with golden hair falling over her closed eyes. She was a porcelain doll letting out the sweetest of snores—snores I'm sure she would deny when she woke up.

Waking up.

My guess was, in a few hours, the sun would rise, and we would finally be able to see six feet down the road and watch skiers brave Holly Hill Peak. The day would start, and we would all continue on from where we'd left off the day before. We'd all have to keep moving forward with our lives, progressing with work and activities, and dates we—maybe—were relieved we'd had to push aside for a little bit.

The laptop sat atop Alice's desk, catching my eye. As if pulling me in its direction, I gently lifted Alice's arm off of me and tip-toed toward it, swiping my finger across the touchpad. Immediately, my inbox at Rom-Com Ready Ventures popped up along with the My Cup o' Joe app hiding behind the screen, snapping me back to reality.

I had two emails asking where the next dating show location would be.

I had three emails asking if we will have any guest companies this season.

I had four emails from possible sponsors as well as two emails from businesses asking to help with the next show to get their brand highlighted.

In a way, I was intrigued with the final two emails.

And then, there was one email...from my brother. I'd sent him a message from this email, explaining the situation to him, and his response made my stomach spin:

I'm glad you're safe. And don't worry about the party. There will be other parties. I mean, the wedding is only a few months away, and that'll be the party of the year. Tell me how the date with Kati goes. She seems like she could be The One for you. Gorgeous, willing to travel, extroverted.

You're not getting any younger, man. Let's get you hooked up and on my level. You deserve it.

I took off my glasses, rubbing my eyes with my palms and taking a deep breath before placing them back on my face.

Though his message was blunt, it wasn't wrong.

I wanted to settle down.

I wanted someone by my side.

And being in my mid-thirties, I knew I had to step it up.

Sighing, I minimized his email and clicked over to the My Cup app. Kati—dark hair cropped at her shoulders, almond-shaped eyes the color of the sky, and a smile that could make anyone melt—appeared beside a new message:

Oh my gosh, I hope you're okay! I'm so sorry about your phone. The weather in Merlin isn't great either, so I'm sure Holly Hill is horrific. Don't drive, and just stay put. But yes, I'd love to meet up at Java Jude's tomorrow at nine. I'm looking soooo forward to finally meeting you in person. Xoxo Kati

Dammit.

Why'd she have to be so sweet?

I looked over my shoulder at Alice—someone I'd learned to be just as sweet, maybe even a little sweeter. Her pink lips were parted slightly as those adorable snores slipped out, her bare chest lifting and falling at such a relaxed speed.

I had to make some choices.

I had to move forward in some way.

Taking a deep breath, I responded to Kati. My fingers tapped the keyboard, and I finally hit send before switching back over to respond to my brother. Once I'd finished doing what I needed to do, I shut the laptop and noticed a stack of sticky notes on the desk beside pink and purple crystals and three pens with little smiley faces at the end.

Grabbing one of the pens and a few sticky notes, I began to write.

CHAPTER FIFTEEN

Alice

SUN SLIPPED THROUGH THE closed curtains of my studio.

Closed.

Had I closed the curtains before falling asleep?

"Ugh..." I mumbled, yawning probably the longest yawn I'd ever yawned. Once my eyes adjusted to the sunshine, I noticed how clear it was outside. A determined snow plow flew up and down the village streets, finally making it safe enough for cars to slowly make their way through town.

I reached to my side and began patting around. "Look, it stopped—"

Then I realized I was only swatting at air.

My hand fell onto the crinkled sheets, Archibald jumping up next to me as if I'd beckoned him. Archibald was lying in the spot where a giant, ginger barbarian had just been lying hours before. Hours before, we'd been rolling around, sweating, and smiling before finally falling asleep only covered in thin sheets.

Had I dreamt it all?

Had Levi-Leo-Leander only been some beautiful character concocted in my mind?

No.

I could smell the cranberry-scented body wash he'd used when he'd showered—walking out in just those damn red boxer briefs...that had matched my red lace panties far too well. The scent covered the pillow next to me along with memories of those boxer briefs and dripping espresso and the cold café counter.

I needed to go sanitize the fuck out of that café before nine o'clock hit.

A flash of purple caught my eye, and I looked toward the door across the room leading to Snowcap Café. A small square was stuck to the door near the handle, and I finally got my ass out of bed, walking toward it with Archibald at my ankles. A sticky note with writing I could barely make out stared up at me. I plucked the note and began reading:

To Alice. I hate that I had to leave this way, but I knew if I stayed, I would have fallen harder. Watching you wake up and bat those eyelashes and snuggle up close would have made me force all obligations aside.

Last night, it felt beyond perfect pushing all those obligations aside and just spending time with you.

I flipped to the back of the sticky note.

The card game, the moment on the counter, the moment by the fire, the moment in bed (there were a lot of moments)...they'll never be forgotten. The same goes for those espresso martinis...that mixologist you were talking about seriously needs to share the wealth. What I'm saying is, thank you. I have some things to figure out, but one thing is for sure—I can't forget the night we had even if I tried. I'd never want to. Love, Leonard-Larson-Larry

Love.

Had he meant to say that?

Of course, I was probably overthinking it. My brain was already overwhelmed to the point of combustion, and this note was only adding to the fire.

Just like everyone else in my damn life, he'd left.

Gone.

Just like my parents. Past boyfriends. Old friends. And soon, Dana would be across the country too.

Just...gone.

I was back to feeling stuck.

And alone.

Archibald meowed at my ankles, and I pressed the note onto the back of the door before picking up the ball of fluff, snuggling him to my chest. "It's just the two of us again, Archie. We'll...we'll be okay. We'll be *great.*"

Meow.

"We have gotten through it all together, and we will get over this emotional night together too."

Meow.

"Let's get out into that damn café and pretend really hard that we're okay," I whispered, walking over to my closet. "It's almost Christmas, after all. Let's pour some fucking joy into the peoples' cups and ignore how empty ours are."

Hiss.

❧❧❧❧❧❧❧❧

I EXPECTED THERE TO be a rush once the snow slowed down, but I didn't expect it to last three days without a break. The snow hadn't fully come to a halt, but the lifted travel ban definitely made people act like there still weren't heavy flakes falling from the sky.

It was as if nothing had ever slowed: people rushing to the mountain, people begging for peppermint mochas—a flavor which I was still waiting to be delivered—people singing Christmas carols, people lighting menorahs, people being overall cheerier than normal.

The highlight of day two of being back in business was overhearing a conversation three customers were having on speaker phone in the corner of the café. I knew one of the customers—a host at a local bed and breakfast—who often knew her visitors well...maybe a little *too* well.

Apparently, that had been the case with the couple she was talking to that day.

The entertainment was a good distraction from the ongoing orders coming in and visions of dark-red hair and darker rimmed glasses popping into my memory.

The third day was as hectic and jolly as the first and second—even jollier because the shipment of peppermint finally arrived, and the snow finally seemed to stop falling.

The fourth day was when Dana rushed into the shop, excited that she was finally closing on a Tudor-style home in Luna Falls, showing me picture after picture. Each photo only made me think about the postcards I'd add to my ever-growing wall of dreams. Even the thought of postcards from Luna Falls made my heart sadden a little bit.

But day five felt different.

It was quieter...calmer. I wasn't sure if that was a blessing or a curse, because my mind kept humming. The quiet only made me think about my cold ass on the café counter and Liam's tongue circling me and his lips humming.

"Did you see this?" Dana asked, one hand slamming onto the counter and her other forcing a phone screen into my face.

I took a step back, both hands lifting with a laugh. "I can't even tell what I'm looking at!"

"It's confirmation of next summer's Rom-Com Ready shows. You know...the ones that inspire all my books—well, sort of. They inspire the sex scenes, if anything."

Rom-Com Ready Ventures.

The shows Liam's company produced.

I hadn't put that together until now.

Reaching for the phone, I swiped across her screen. "It's...going to be in Merlin?"

"On Claus Lake! Isn't that *insane*?!" Dana was completely losing her shit over this—hands climbing through her dark hair with her eyes practically bulging out of her face. "Maybe I won't move after all and audition for the show—just for research purposes, of course."

"I think that's the best damn idea I've ever heard." I was nodding so hard my neck was beginning to ache.

Laughing, Dana said, "Why don't *you* audition for the show? It's an hour away, and you could just shut the café for a couple months or hire—"

"Dana…" I whispered, my head nods slowly turning into head shakes side to side. "You know I can't. I have to keep the coffee shop going."

"You can."

The hushed voice forced both of our heads to snap toward the front door.

Where a tall man stood.

Light eyes.

Dark-rimmed glasses.

Auburn hair.

"Liam?" I stepped around the counter slowly, trailing my hand along the cold wooden top until I stepped beside Dana, who stood with her jaw agape. "You're…you're back."

Liam took a step forward, shaking some snowflakes from his hair until he was about three feet from me.

Three feet.

Damn, we'd quickly broken that rule the other night.

"I needed another dirty chai latte." He smiled, the tiniest dimple peeking through his five o'clock shadow. "I want to make sure the barista remembers my name."

"I don't think she could ever forget it," I whispered, taking a small step forward before stopping myself and cocking my head to the side. "Why are you *really* here, though? Did your date not go well?"

Dana scoffed next to us, taking a step back with crossed arms as she just watched us like one of the Rom-Com Ready shows.

Or maybe as inspiration.

Liam immediately raised his hands, palms facing me. "Whoa, whoa, whoa. We're going right to *that*?"

"Yes," I stated confidently. "Yes, we are."

"The date...it didn't happen," Liam admitted, scratching his neck and looking down at his...jeans? Was he wearing blue jeans? And was a sweater hiding beneath his puffer jacket?

Who was this man standing in front of me without his power suit?

I pressed my lips together, nodding my head slowly in response. "Did she...not show?"

Liam shook his head, taking another step forward. *Two feet.* "We both showed, but...I couldn't stay. I couldn't follow through with the date and had to tell her in person why."

My brow furrowed. "Why...why couldn't you stay?"

Liam stepped closer. *One foot.* "Because she wasn't *you*, Alice."

My heart fell through my feet.

My stomach spun in circles.

Had I heard him correctly?

"But she would fit into your life perfectly. I...I can't—"

Liam cupped my chin and lifted it slightly, doing this right as I was about to look away, forcing our gazes together. "Don't say it. You can do what you want and go where your heart wants you to...and you can do this while keeping your family's vision going."

"Liam...you know I can't—"

"What if I said you could go to Merlin Isle on Claus Lake with us for our next show and be our sponsored coffee shop?"

What the *fuck*?

How?

"Because I'm in charge and make the rules," Liam laughed.

Oh, I'd said those thoughts out loud.

"But...how? And why?"

"We were trying to incorporate local businesses into next season's show, and after meeting up with Kati—after I realized she wasn't who I was looking for—I thought about *you*. It made me go find that espresso martini aficionado you like. Since she co-owns Mage Hand Martinis in Merlin, she may also come on as a highlighted local business. Java Jude's and Spellbound Beans are joining as well—each corner of the island will have a coffee hut."

"You found *Margot*?" I asked, blinking quickly—shocked. "She's, like, my idol."

"I know, and now you can meet her and work alongside her for two months...while still keeping the Snowcap Café name going. You'll just be doing it on a gorgeous little island on the lake."

My brain was spinning a million miles a minute.

And thank God a customer hadn't walked in, because if they had, I would have completely ignored them.

I...I didn't hate this idea.

The chance to escape—to travel—while keeping the Snowcap brand strong would be a dream.

And during the slow season, nonetheless.

"Al..." Dana said, her hand falling onto my shoulder. "You can't *not* do this."

"She's right," Liam interjected, smiling.

Damn, that smile.

I'd seen it so much over the course of our night together.

And the chance to see even more of it set my entire body on fire.

My entire *soul*.

"I...yeah...um..." I said, his hands running down my arms until they wrapped around my waist, pulling me in close. With a palm flat against his chest, I twisted my wrist to grab some of his jacket and pulled him closer, pressing my lips to his. His heat illuminated me, bringing energy to parts of me that had been ice cold for the last five days.

For the last three *years*.

He released his soft lips, pressing his forehead against mine. "So, what do you say, *Alicia*?"

I couldn't stop the snort from escaping my lips, my head falling back with a laugh that felt so damn good to free. "I'm saying yes, Lester. Right now, I'm definitely saying yes."

And then his lips hit mine again, and I got lost in the taste of his tongue against my own, the feel of his hand making its way to the back of my neck, and the press of his hips to mine.

Dana scratched her head, cocking it to the side. "Wait...who is Alicia?"

Epilogue

LIAM

"**A**ND THEN YOU JUST add a little bit of chocolate liqueur...but it *has* to be *this* brand."

Alice reached for the bottle in Margot's hands. Squinting down at it, Alice laughed, "Oh my goodness, how cute. It's *really* called Kickass Kocoa?"

"It sure as fuck is! You can only use the best when making these," Margot said, setting the bottle back on the counter. "It's all we use at Mage Hand. We have to put up with gamers here regularly...so, they need their asses kicked both in their games and out. I say this as a gamer myself."

"No wonder our martinis tasted weird. We didn't have shots of Kickass Kocoa in them," I said, lifting an eyebrow and peering over at Alice, who threw me a savage look.

"*Excuse* me, but I'm pretty sure you *loved* those martinis, sir."

I had.

It was as if she'd added an aphrodisiac to them.

I mean, the leftovers ended up strewn across my body.

"I kid, I kid." I leaned forward against the bar, reaching for the top of her head and ruffling her beautiful blonde hair separated into two perfect braids with little beads intertwined throughout. "You saw what they did to me that night."

Margot paused from behind the bar of the speakeasy—a small space she worked out of in the back of a comic book and gaming shop in Merlin Heights. She and her sister had truly made what looked like a large closet into a space perfect for long nights of tabletop games with a side of *very* strong espresso martinis. She'd become known in Merlin Heights for her recipe—and overall persona: tough, bold, outspoken. So, when I'd found her three months earlier, I knew she and Alice would hit it off.

I mean, Alice was now leaning into mixologist country after agreeing to help out at the Mage Hand hut as well as the Snowcap hut during the show. Before I knew it, she'd be switching gears completely and turning Snowcap Café into an espresso bar.

But that was a dream for another time.

A dream I could absolutely see Alice following through with.

She had so many of them. Dreams. She'd stopped chasing them the moment her parents passed away, deciding to chase *their* dreams instead. She'd felt so guilty even thinking about what she wanted to do and where she wanted to go that she'd trapped herself in a bubble for years. A bubble she enjoyed, but one that trapped her nonetheless.

I was grateful to help her pop that bubble.

"Here...try this one." Margot placed a martini in front of both Alice and me. Alice wrapped her ringed fingers around the stem, lifting it into the air to clink against mine. Right before she was about to bring the glass to her lips, Margot said, "No, shit...wait!"

She twisted on her heel, wisps of short, teal hair falling in front of her face as she grabbed a mason jar out of a cabinet. Grinning a smile that curled to one side of her face, she set the jar between us. "I do something different when it comes to topping the drink with the espresso beans." Margot reached into the mason jar, plucking out three beans. "Grab three beans to sprinkle on top of the drink. With the first two, make two wishes...don't tell anyone. With the final bean, tell us a battle you're excited to win."

"A battle?" I asked, lifting an eyebrow as Alice practically dove into the mason jar, snagging three beans.

"Yeah, a battle." After Alice placed three beans in her palm, Margot slid the glass closer to me. "We tried to make it something fun for customers since most of them come here to play Dungeons and Dragons. So, battles are involved. But this battle can be physical or mental or something actually happening in your life that you're looking forward to conquering. Battles don't always have to be negative. Sometimes, they're just little roadblocks in the way of where your heart is leading you."

"Like...a task we're excited to complete?" Alice asked, shaking the beans in her hand.

"Exactly!" Margot shouted, tattooed fingers plucking three beans out for herself. "For me, I'm helping my sister plan her wedding...and that's going to be one hell of a battle. So, I'm excited—and terrified as fuck—to help her with that."

"That's fair. Weddings can be scary!" Alice said.

"You think so?" I asked, fumbling with the beans in my palm. "I thought you'd be someone who likes weddings. I mean, you're going to my brother's next month. You were ecstatic about that."

Alice shrugged, looking down into her drink. "I do like them...and I am excited for your brother's wedding. I just haven't thought about how mine will look without my parents there. I just would miss their energy...miss their love."

Love.

Alice's future wedding would be filled to the brink with love—I just knew it.

Her parents' energy would flow alongside her with every sweep across the dance floor, and she'd hear them with every laugh echoing throughout the room.

I leaned forward, bringing my finger to Alice's chin and tipping her face toward mine. "Their love will be everywhere at your wedding someday. Their love and your love and the love everyone has for you. It will be everywhere."

"How do you know that, Liam?"

My name.

Whenever she said my actual name, there was a reason.

And I saw this as reason enough to push through a little mental battle I'd been fighting lately.

One small, little battle rumbling in my head out of nervousness.

Stepping back, I brought one tiny bean between my index finger and thumb. Closing my eyes tight, I made a wish and dropped it into the espresso martini, doing the same with the second. When it came to the third bean, I opened my eyes and looked directly at Alice.

Damn, she was a beauty.

"I wouldn't call this a battle as much as I'll call it something I've wanted to say for a while...but haven't had the courage to until now." I placed the bean, not on the drink but onto the counter. With that, I poured out a small pile of beans, Margot and Alice just watching as I plucked them out and set them on the counter in specific places.

"You know you're going to be the one to clean this shit up, right?" Margot stated monotonously, dropping her first bean into her drink after closing her eyes for two quick seconds.

Nodding, I continued to shift the beans around on the counter.

Alice wrapped her hand around my forearm, shaking her head with a laugh. "What are you—"

And then she paused, her hand releasing from my arm as she stepped back.

In front of her—in front of us—were the words *I love you* spelled out in espresso beans.

Her hand flew to her mouth, and she immediately met my gaze—a gaze becoming a bit blurry from unexpected tears. Dammit, I hadn't expected to cry—or tear up, for that matter. I'd never said these words aloud before, and still, I hadn't—I'd spelled them out. But I'd known Alice for long enough—even just it being three months—to know she was *The One*.

She was the one *I* wanted to marry someday.

She was the one I wanted to play silly card games with until late at night.

She was the one I wanted to snuggle with while her cat hissed at us from across the room.

She was *The One* I wanted to be with for the rest of my life.

"Liam...you...you really mean it?"

Margot dropped another bean into her drink as she looked between the two of us.

I twisted the final bean between my fingers, smiling. "Of course I do. We spent a lifetime together during that snowy night. I can't imagine going the rest of my life without you. I'm in love with you, Alice. I've never said that to anyone, which was why I chose it as my third espresso bean. And you know what? It feels so damn good pushing through that nervous battle. The look on your face says it all."

A tear dripped down her flushed cheeks, and she immediately brought the back of her hand up to wipe it away. Her bottom lip trembled, and she stepped forward, pressing her palm to my cheek. "Liam. I love you so, so much."

I dropped the third bean into the martini and cupped the sides of her face, pulling her in until her lips pressed against mine. Fire shot through my body as my tongue swiped against hers, her hips flush to mine as she wrapped her hands around my waist.

It felt like it had that first night three months ago.

It felt new, exciting, and a little scary too.

But one thing was for sure...it felt so damn right.

Read All of the Holly Hill Winter Novella Collection!

About the Author

JENNIFER ALINE writes stories that combine the steamy elements of romance with the raw realities of friendship and family-focused themes of women's fiction. She loves creating quirky characters with big personalities who are forced to challenge themselves and step outside their comfort zone...while also finding love—or something like it—along the way.

Jennifer lives in Western New York with her twin daughters and grumpy miniature schnauzer. She has an unhealthy obsession with vintage typewriters, owns way too many plants, and is a self-titled coffee snob. When she isn't writing, reading, or chasing her daughters around, she can be found singing karaoke, taking dance classes, or searching for the newest local coffee shop to obsess over.

Also Written by Jennifer Aline

The Ex Project: A Merlin Heights Book

The Naked Book Club: A Merlin Heights Book